Blond, blue-eyed

Mike caught sight of Charlie and as if on cue, his leg started to ache.... The pain reminded him of the night he'd been wounded in the line of duty.

In his book, trouble, Charlie and his aching leg were synonymous. He wasn't afraid of what she might do next; he *was* afraid of a loose cannon, and that description custom-fit Charlie Norris to a T.

There was another concern, Mike thought uneasily as he made his way through the crowded room. He was way too fascinated with Charlie for his own good. It just might prove a fatal attraction in his line of work as an agent in the Secret Service...because Charlie Norris was a magnet for trouble!

Dear Reader,

Millionaire. Prince. Secret agent. Doctor. If any—or all—of these men strike your fancy, well…you're in luck! These fabulous guys are waiting for you in the pages of this month's offerings from Harlequin American Romance.

His best friend's request to father her child leads millionaire Gabe Deveraux to offer a bold marriage proposal in *My Secret Wife* by Cathy Gillen Thacker, the latest installment of THE DEVERAUX LEGACY series. A royal request makes Prince Jace Carradigne heir to a throne—and in search of his missing fiancée—in Mindy Neff's *The Inconveniently Engaged Prince*, part of our ongoing series THE CARRADIGNES: AMERICAN ROYALTY. (And there are royals galore to be found when the series comes to a sensational ending in *Heir to the Throne*, a special two-in-one collection by Kasey Michaels and Carolyn Davidson, available next month wherever Harlequin books are sold.)

Kids, kangaroos and a kindhearted woman are all in a day's work for cool and collected secret agent Mike Wheeler in *Secret Service Dad*, the second book in Mollie Molay's GROOMS IN UNIFORM series. And a big-city doctor attempts to hide his true identity—and his affections—for a Montana beauty in *The Doctor Wore Boots* by Debra Webb, the conclusion to the TRADING PLACES duo.

So be sure to catch all of these wonderful men this month—and every month—as you enjoy their wonderful love stories from Harlequin American Romance.

Happy reading,

Melissa Jeglinski
Associate Senior Editor
Harlequin American Romance

SECRET SERVICE DAD
Mollie Molay

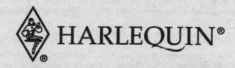

HARLEQUIN®

TORONTO • NEW YORK • LONDON
AMSTERDAM • PARIS • SYDNEY • HAMBURG
STOCKHOLM • ATHENS • TOKYO • MILAN • MADRID
PRAGUE • WARSAW • BUDAPEST • AUCKLAND

To June Arias for introducing me to the world of kangaroos. If there are any errors, they are solely mine. Thank you.

ISBN 0-373-16947-7

SECRET SERVICE DAD

Copyright © 2002 by Mollie Molé.

Visit us at www.eHarlequin.com

Printed in U.S.A.

ABOUT THE AUTHOR

After working for a number of years as a logistics contract administrator in the aircraft industry, Mollie Molay turned to a career she found far more satisfying—writing romance novels. Mollie lives in Northridge, California, surrounded by her two daughters and eight grandchildren, many of whom find their way into her books. She enjoys hearing from her readers and welcomes comments. You can write to her at Harlequin Books, 300 East 42nd St., 6th Floor, New York, NY 10017.

Books by Mollie Molay

HARLEQUIN AMERICAN ROMANCE

560—FROM DRIFTER TO DADDY
597—HER TWO HUSBANDS
616—MARRIAGE BY MISTAKE
638—LIKE FATHER, LIKE SON
682—NANNY & THE BODYGUARD
703—OVERNIGHT WIFE
729—WANTED: DADDY
776—FATHER IN TRAINING
799—DADDY BY CHRISTMAS
815—MARRIED BY MIDNIGHT
839—THE GROOM CAME C.O.D.
879—BACHELOR-AUCTION BRIDEGROOM
897—THE BABY IN THE BACK SEAT
938—THE DUCHESS & HER BODYGUARD*
947—SECRET SERVICE DAD*

*Grooms in Uniform

ALL-POINTS BULLETIN

The following fugitive is wanted by the
MᴄLᴇᴀɴ, Vɪʀɢɪɴɪᴀ, Pᴏʟɪᴄᴇ Dᴇᴘᴀʀᴛᴍᴇɴᴛ

Wᴀɴᴛᴇᴅ

"Boomer" Norris
(aka "Joey")

Norris is unarmed, but can turn overly affectionate if cornered.
He has been on the run since escaping from the private zoo owned by
Charlene "Charlie" Norris earlier this week. If you have any information
regarding this individual or have knowledge of his whereabouts, please contact
Sergeant Hawkins of the minor crime support division,
McLean Police Department.

Prologue

Europe, the Country of Baronovia, February

Flailing helplessly, U.S. Secret Service agent Mike Wheeler tumbled to the ground. Moments before, he'd been idly checking out security measures around the palace where the wedding of Duchess Mary Louise to Commander Wade Stevens of the U.S. Navy was to take place in a few hours. Now, he was lying on his back in a bed of carefully tended petunias and staring up into a pair of startled blue eyes.

"Oh no! I'm so sorry! I'm afraid I wasn't looking where I was going. Are you okay? Here, let me help you up!" A pair of manicured feminine hands pulled at his tuxedo jacket.

Mike bit back the paralyzing pain in his injured leg and grimly eyed his attacker, Charlie Norris, a fellow American and a member of the wedding party. She was the last person he wanted to meet.

He took a deep breath and struggled to his feet. Getting shot in the line of duty three months ago had been the pits. Getting knocked over by the woman who inadvertently had played a large part in the events that had led to the shooting didn't make the pain any easier to bear.

"Are you sure you don't need any help?" She took a corner of her silk stole, wet it between her lips and tried to scrub something off his chin.

To his chagrin, whether he approved of her or not, his body warmed at her touch. And tightened at the sight of full, tempting lips so close to his own. He grabbed her hand before things could become more personal.

"Thank you, no," he said tightly. "Give me a minute. I'll be fine."

She waited hopefully, her concern evident. Considering how he felt about the way trouble seemed to follow Charlie and wind up affecting him, he would have been just as happy to see her leave.

"I understand that there are over two hundred rooms in the palace and that it is surrounded by hundreds of acres of grounds," he said when he could breath freely again. "How did you manage to pick precisely the same two square feet of ground I was standing on to stumble about on?"

She colored. "I'm afraid I wasn't thinking."

"That's the problem," he agreed as he tried to balance himself squarely on two feet. He hadn't approved of the lady's methods as the concierge of Blair House even before she ignored security rules to aid and abet the forbidden courtship and subsequent fairy-tale marriage of today's unlikely bride and groom. He didn't approve of her any more now.

Charlie bristled. She had been about to tell Mike she'd barreled into him simply because she had slipped down the sloping lawn. "The only mistake I made was to head for the only friendly face I thought I recognized out here," she said. "Strike the word *friendly*. And furthermore," she went on as she tried to balance on one foot, "it looks as if I've sprained my ankle. All you have to show for this accident are a few grass stains!" Turning to leave, she teetered and flailed at empty air.

Instinctively, Mike reached to catch Charlie before she fell. Too late—she stumbled, squealed and, to his discomfort, landed squarely in his arms.

He closed his eyes and mentally counted to ten. However misguided Charlie Norris might be, and no matter how wary he was of what she might do next, she was every bit as soft and warm as he'd been afraid she would turn out to be.

Chapter One

It was said by some that Washington's Blair House was jinxed.

Now that it looked as if a second State Department guest within six months had become the target of a disgruntled foreign nationalist, Secret Service agent Mike Wheeler was prepared to believe the rumor. At least this shooting, thank God, hadn't happened on his watch.

For some reason, whenever Mike thought of Blair House, his thoughts turned to the Blair House concierge, Charlene Norris, dubbed Charlie by all who knew her. She was trouble, blond, blue-eyed trouble. If that wasn't bad enough, she usually got him involved in whatever trouble she managed to get herself into.

His fears had been realized when he reported for duty that day. The foyer of the residence was teeming with activity. The air smelled of cordite. Cell phones were ringing. Sirens screamed outside, Secret Service agents, anyone with the credentials to get in the front door milled around the reception room where, to his dismay, it looked as if another attempted assassination had taken place.

His practiced eye took in a wounded man who lay sprawled, groaning on the marble entry floor clutching his bleeding shoulder. An agitated man dressed in a foreign military uniform stood handcuffed in the custody of two D.C. policemen. The cuffed man was protesting at the top of his lungs, but the police seemed to be ignoring their suspect. One D.C. lawman gingerly held a smoking gun by two fingers while a third was preparing to fit the gun into a plastic evidence bag.

Off to the side, six uniformed staff members stood gaping at the scene being played out in front of them. Mike didn't blame them. He could hardly believe it himself.

He cut through the mob scene until he caught sight of Charlie Norris. She looked as if she was in a state of shock. There was blood on one of her wrists and on the skirt of her tailored beige suit. He was concerned at the sight, but not surprised. He'd had the sinking feeling that somehow she would be in the thick of any action, hadn't he?

And not for the first time.

As if on cue, his leg started to ache. The pain

reminded him of the night a disenchanted Baronovian nationalist had attempted to assassinate Prince Alexis of Baronovia and his daughter, the duchess Mary Louise, the night he'd been wounded in the line of duty.

In his book, trouble, Charlie and his aching leg were synonymous.

He wasn't actually afraid of what she might do next. Almost half his size, he could have handled two of her. Besides, problem-solving was his job. What he *was* afraid of was a loose cannon, a description that custom-fit Charlie Norris to a T.

There was another concern, he thought uneasily as he made his way through the crowded room to where the shooting had taken place. He was too fascinated with Charlie for his own good. A fatal attraction if there ever was one, he thought unhappily.

Gazing at Charlie today, he realized that Charlie Norris, the coltish figure from the Baronovia caper, obviously was a magnet for trouble. Her hair was summer sunbeams, her eyes the color of clear blue summer skies. Used as a weapon, à la the famed Helen of Troy, her blue eyes could have sunk a thousand battleships. But instead of her usual professional, tailored appearance, tonight she looked distraught and disheveled.

Normally, Charlie had the most sinful and inviting smile he'd ever encountered on a woman. And, to his professional way of thinking, the darndest way of talking herself out of any problem she managed to get herself into. She wasn't smiling now. After a glance around at the chaotic activity, he couldn't blame her.

He bit back his frustration as he came up along her side. To his chagrin, his body reminded him he hadn't been with a woman for a while; not since before the Baronovian shooting. Why in the hell he remembered this now, in a room full of people that resembled a scene out of a TV mystery comedy, beat the hell out of him. Maybe it was the excitement of the moment—he always seemed to feel high when danger threatened. If that weren't so, he never would have joined the Secret Service nor would he have met Charlie.

Mike ground to a halt and turned his gaze on her. From the distressed expression on her face, he knew she had to have been present when all hell had broken loose.

"What?" she said before he could open his mouth. She glared at him from under narrowed eyebrows and crossed her arms in front of her as if to put some distance between them. She certainly didn't look pleased to see him. Maybe it was difficult for her to read his opinion of the situation.

He might have been more surprised at her question, if he'd been paying closer attention. The truth was, he'd been so busy admiring the dimple on her left cheek he hadn't been concentrating.

Wrong.

He knew better than most that the best defense, when you've painted yourself into a corner, was a good offense. After his experience with Charlie in Baronovia, he knew firsthand she was damn good at the offensive end of the game. To complicate matters, she made him feel guilty for not trusting her even when he had nothing to feel guilty about.

"Wheeler! Over here!" a loud voice cut through the noise and confusion.

Mike glanced over to where several Secret Service men and women were huddled in conference. His assistant gestured for him to come over. "In a minute," he called, then turned back to Charlie. "What happened here?"

She glared at him, her blue eyes blazing. "You mean, what did I have to do with it, don't you?"

"You've got it." Damn, that fierce look cooled any sexual fantasies he might have entertained. Just as well. Another thing he'd learned the hard way was that it was never wise to fraternize with the people you worked with. It didn't look as if she were interested in fraternizing, anyway. If looks could freeze, he would have been an icicle by now. He jammed his hands into his pockets and waited for the fur to fly.

"Nothing. Absolutely nothing," she said and gestured to the handcuffed swarthy man who by now had lost his voice and was glowering at her. "All I did was introduce General Negri here, to Mr. Ober-hammer of the visiting United Nations' contingent over there.'' She gestured to a man who lay on the marble floor in the entryway. ''At the general's request, I might add.''

''That's all that happened?''

''No,'' she answered breathlessly. ''That was only the beginning. The general pulled a gun. At first I thought it had to be joke.''

''A joke?'' Mike glanced over at the gun. ''That doesn't look like a toy gun to me.''

She plastered her hands on her hips before he got any further. ''How was I to know the man was going to start shooting?''

Mike glanced at the man who lay moaning on the marble floor. ''Have you called 911?''

''Of course. That's part of my job.''

Mike nodded curtly. From his previous experiences with Charlie, he had the feeling she wrote her job description as she went along. As for the wounded man, from the look of things, he would keep until the paramedics arrived. ''Anyone else get hurt?''

''Well,'' she went on, brushing her hand across her forehead, seemingly unaware her wrist was bleeding. ''I guess you could say so.'' She aimed a shaking finger at a ceramic bas relief sculpture over the mantel that depicted a trio of angels holding hands and dancing across a cloud-filled sky. A bullet hole was visible where one of the angel's belly button would have been. "*He* took the other bullet."

"Get real," he snapped to keep himself from laughing. Where else but here would a plaster angel have taken a bullet in its belly button? On the other hand, it wasn't all that had happened. The bullet had apparently grazed Charlie's hand in passing. "This is serious."

"Yes, I know," she said in a shaking voice. "I couldn't believe it myself. But it's true. I tried to grab the gun when I realized things were getting serious." She stopped to catch her breath. "Anyway, it's a little late to get upset about it now, isn't it?"

"You haven't learned much since the last time you set fire to a powder keg, have you?" Mike growled. He pulled a fresh white handkerchief from his back pocket and wrapped it around her right wrist. Thank goodness she was shaken enough to let him do it.

"You *could* have checked the guy's credentials before you made the introduction," he went on, surprised at the tender feeling that came over him as he wrapped the makeshift bandage around her slender wrist. That was Charlie all right. A mixed bag of sensuality and danger.

"It's my job to introduce guests to each other, Mr. Wheeler, not to interrogate or to search them," she retorted. "Among other things, I *am* the official hostess here. It says so in the fine print of my contract.''

Mike gave up. If Charlie hadn't learned by now how to run a tight ship, nothing he could say was going to change her.

The alternative was to keep a close eye on her. To see to it she stopped trusting anyone who came along with some innocent request or another. Especially if they wore the uniform of a foreign country.

Somehow the prospect of watching over Charlie didn't seem to bother him as much as it might have—if only he'd had his head on straight. Hell, he'd be the first to admit that she drove him nuts at the same time she fascinated the hell out of him. Without her, his job as the Blair House Special-Agent-in-Charge would have been boring as hell.

Not that he was looking for excitement. At thirty-five, he was looking forward to a peaceful period in his life. At least until his son Jake reached puberty.

"Don't leave the premises," he said and turned away. "I may want to talk to you later."

"That's what you think," she answered. She gestured to the splatter of blood on her beige skirt. "I'm going home to change as soon as I can get out of here. And as for you, Mr. Wheeler, I don't care if I never lay eyes on you again."

To her chagrin, Mike winked and went on his way.

She grimly watched him stride over to the group waiting for him. If ever a man had the ability to get under her skin, it was this take-charge, go-by-the-book, stuffy Mike Wheeler. A man who apparently had never forgiven her for passing Commander Wade Stevens's address to Prince Alexis's turncoat bodyguard months ago. How was she to have known the man had been out to kidnap the prince's daughter, Mary Louise? Or that an attempted assassination of the prince would follow?

She would have really been annoyed with Mike Wheeler tonight, if, heaven help her, she weren't so attracted to him.

His hair, cut in the approved military style, topped a fit body that had to be the result of daily trips to the Blair House gym. As if that weren't enough to feed his ego, he was tall, dark and, except for the scar at the side of his chin, handsome. Handsome enough to interest any woman foolish enough to fall for a lawman.

As for the Secret Service, from what she had observed in the two years she'd been working as the Blair House concierge, the profession was not only dangerous and demanding, it took all of a man's time and attention, and sometimes his life. With her late father as an example, she didn't want any part of it.

Not that she knew much about Mike. If he had

any kind of a home life, she wasn't aware of it. He kept his private life, what there was of it, to himself.

Which somehow seemed to make him more of a challenge.

She shook the cobwebs out of her mind. She would do well to remember that she wasn't prepared to fall in love with any man she'd kiss goodbye in the morning and suffer the uncertainty of not knowing if he would live to come back to her at night. She never wanted to suffer as her mother had after her policeman father had been killed attempting to foil a bank robbery.

She wasn't going to let herself fall in love with a lawman. Not even if he managed to make her hormones snap to attention whenever she laid eyes on him.

No way.

What really irked the heck out of her was the realization that he acted as if she couldn't be relied on.

"Sorry to bother you at a time like this, Miss Norris," a voice broke into her dark thoughts. "There's a man out front who says he wants to talk to you."

Charlie swung around to face Henry Ochoa, the Blair House doorman. Too frustrated with her mixed emotions over Mike's evident low opinion of her to be polite, she snapped, "Too bad. Right now, there isn't a man alive *I* want to talk to."

Startled, the doorman took a step backward and cleared his throat. "But Miss Norris," he stammered. "He says he's Commander Daniel O'Hara from JAG. Since he's wearing the uniform of a United States naval officer, I guess I have to believe him."

Dan O'Hara! Of course! Commander Wade Stevens's fellow lawyer at JAG and the best man at the recent wedding in Baronovia.

"Let him in, please." She took a deep breath and tried to pull herself together. No way was she going to let Mike's opinion of her make a difference in how she thought of herself. She was comfortable with herself and that was all that mattered. "He might turn out to be the only intelligent man around here I can talk to."

Suddenly, the scene around her erupted in chaos as the general suddenly tried to wrestle his way out of custody. "I have diplomatic immunity, I tell you!" the distraught man shouted. "You cannot hold me against my will!"

"Unfortunately, the man is right," Dan O'Hara muttered under his breath as he joined Charlie. "He doesn't even have to make a statement if he doesn't want to." He paused to look at the numerous men in black and uniformed D.C. police milling around the room. "What kind of trouble did you manage to get yourself into this time?"

Charlie's zero opinion of men immediately extended to O'Hara. What had happened to "innocent until proven guilty"?

"You too, Dan? What's with you men? Why does it always have to be something *I* did?"

Seemingly unabashed, O'Hara grinned. "Maybe because I know how deeply you were involved the last time hell broke out around here?"

Charlie glared her frustration. "As I told Mike Wheeler, I was just doing my job back then. Just as I was trying to do it today. Can I help it if things don't always go as planned?"

"If you say so." Dan gazed around the foyer. "Say, who's in charge around here, anyway?"

"Wheeler, but he's busy right now," Charlie answered with a frown as the general recovered his voice and began to rant and rave again. "Since you're a lawyer, maybe you can do something with the general over there."

"Thanks, but no thanks," Dan laughed. "I'm a JAG lawyer, United States Navy, period. This is State Department business. I just dropped by to deliver a message from Wade and the duchess."

"How is May doing?" Charlie thought back to the time when JAG Commander Wade Stevens and the Dowager Duchess of Lorrania, then a guest of the U.S. government, had met at a diplomatic function. And she remembered the fur that had flown between them before they realized they were meant for each other. If Stevens and his duchess had managed to find each other in spite of a similar, if not worse, mess than she found herself in now, then maybe there was some hope to get Mike to listen to reason.

"May asked me to tell you she's deliriously happy. And that she and Wade expect to be back in D.C. in a couple of weeks."

Charlie considered Dan for a long moment. The frantic activity surrounding her faded into the background as the past flashed through her mind. Wade Stevens and May Baron *had* had a rocky relationship until May had managed to change Wade for the better. Maybe that's what it would take to turn a robot like Mike into a feeling man; a woman who was interested and determined enough to humanize him. And maybe even to save the man from himself. If ever there was a man who needed saving, she thought sourly, it was Mike Wheeler. "Really? So you're saying JAG commanders can be tamed."

Dan shrugged and grinned sheepishly. "Yeah, but you have to shoot them first to get their attention."

"Really?" Charlie gazed over to where Mike was now briefing the new crew reporting for night duty. His all-business, take-charge attitude might be okay for them, but it wasn't for her.

One thing she did know, Mike's attitude about women left something to be desired. She wasn't going to put up with it any longer. It was time to show Mike he was as human as the next man. And to find a way to show him that no matter what he thought about her methods of operation, there was nothing wrong with her. Even if her why-not attitude apparently drove him up a wall.

If getting a man shot was a requirement or prelude to taming him, she mused as she watched Mike limp back to her, at least she was halfway home.

She absentmindedly thanked Dan for delivering the message from the duchess. If he only knew, he'd also delivered another, more interesting message; a Secret Service agent could undoubtedly be tamed by the same means the duchess had used on her JAG lawyer. And Charlie felt she was just the woman to do it.

"O'Hara?" Mike held out his hand. "Haven't seen you since the wedding. How you doing?"

"Better than you, from what I've heard." Dan grinned as Charlie sniffed and left to speak to the paramedics.

Mike raised an inquiring eyebrow. "Come again?"

"I was thinking about how you and Charlie seldom saw eye-to-eye during the Baronovia caper. Doesn't look as if much has changed since then, has it?"

"If you're talking about my reaction to Charlie's idea of a Frisbee contest in an unguarded park with the duchess's safety at stake, you've got that right," Mike said after a glance to make sure Charlie was out of hearing. "The lady has a knack for acting before thinking."

Dan grinned. "From the way you look at her it hasn't prevented you from falling for her."

"You've got that right, too," Mike agreed. "But I'll be damned if I understand why when she attracts trouble the way a cat attracts fleas."

Dan smothered a laugh and turned to leave. "If anyone can handle Charlie, I have a feeling you're the man to do it."

"Not if I can help it," Mike muttered.

Charlie came back in time to hear him. "Did you have something else to say, Mr. Wheeler?"

Mike glanced at her. Mr. Wheeler? She was back to the best-offense-is-the-best-defense position that fried him. "No. Talk to you later."

Charlie frowned when Mike walked away. The man was a puzzle, all right. But, first things first, she mused as she set her mind back to the business at hand. There was a wounded man waiting to be taken to the emergency hospital. There was also the shooter, whom the FBI was going to have to debrief. And, to her annoyance, there was Mike wanting to know more about the shooting incident after she'd already told him everything she knew.

Her first opportunity to do something about turning Mike into a more reasonable man would have to wait until Sunday. A day when she'd volunteered her place for a do-it-yourself Blair House picnic.

Surely by then they would have a chance to talk to each other like two reasonable people. The only problem was that every time they got together, something major seemed to happen to Mike.

All she had to do was make sure Mike wouldn't come to harm in the process of taming him, she thought with a guilty twinge of conscience as he limped away. What could possibly go wrong at a picnic?

Squaring her jaw, Charlie turned back to matters at hand. She wasn't interested in winning Mike for herself, mind you, but showing Mike he was as human as the next person could be interesting. No matter how she looked at it, taming Mike Wheeler was going to be a job and a half.

Chapter Two

Matters didn't improve between them when Mike arrived unannounced in Charlie's office the next morning. He carried a sheaf of papers in his hand and had a determined look in his eyes. Ordinarily, she wouldn't have minded, but at the moment he was the last person on earth she cared to entertain in her office. If he discovered what was going on in here, coupled with the negative image he already had of her, her professional reputation wasn't worth a plugged nickel. Not that it mattered, she told herself, the man's attitude was enough to try a saint.

"What are you doing here, Mike?"

He looked taken aback at her attitude. His eyes narrowed, an eyebrow rose. "I work here, remember?"

"Of course," she said, brushing aside her instinctive reaction to his unexpected and definitely unwanted appearance. Forcing a smile, she risked a glance at the coatrack behind him. "Actually, I meant, what are you doing here in my office this morning?''

"I need to get a few more details about the shooting yesterday. I didn't come back right away because you looked a little queasy and in no condition to talk.'' He gestured to her bandaged wrist. ''Feeling a little better this morning?''

"I'm fine, it was only a scratch," Charlie answered, more and more uneasy at his presence with every passing moment. Considering the state of affairs between them, and what was going on in her office, she didn't feel very well, at that. Too bad she hadn't had the foresight to close the office door behind her.

Their gazes locked. She could tell he sensed something was wrong with her. It looked as if the visit was going to end in a standoff, until, to her dismay, a strange guttural sound broke the silence.

Mike cocked his head and looked around the office for the source. ''What was that?''

"What was what? I didn't hear anything.'' The feeble smile froze on Charlie's lips as the sound came again. The unthinkable was about to happen. She silently prayed that the sound wouldn't be repeated.

"I'm sure I heard something," Mike glanced cautiously around the office again, finally shrugged and took a seat by her desk. ''Maybe it was my imagination. Got the time to answer a few questions?''

"Actually, no." She summoned her best smile and remained beside the open office door. Maybe he would take the broad hint and leave. "I have a full morning ahead today. How about tomorrow?"

The sound came again. This time, too loud for her to ignore. She frantically tried to think of a sensible explanation for the sound, but her mind seemed to have turned to mush. Any way she looked at it, she was knee-deep in trouble—and with the last man in the world she wanted to be in trouble with. He'd already as much as told her she was one card short of a full deck. What would he think of her now?

She followed Mike's gaze to the large cloth tote bag she'd hung on the coatrack this morning. To her deepening dismay, it was shaking as if something inside was doing a rumba, with sound effects to match.

"Maybe I'm nuts," Mike said as he got to his feet and cautiously eyed the shaking tote bag, "but it looks to me as if there's something alive in there." He paused and fixed her with a grim look that sent her heart skidding down to her toes. "You wouldn't happen to know what it is, would you?"

Charlie swallowed hard. There *was* something alive in the tote bag. How could she deny the truth when it was so blatantly obvious? She debated the alternatives and finally decided she had to give Mike some kind of story to throw him offtrack before he looked inside the bag for himself. But then, she thought as she took a deep breath, this was no ordinary situation.

To add to her present problem, she was all too aware this wasn't going to do much for her reputation.

"It's only Boomer," she said finally when she tried and failed to come up with a decent story. She patted the tote bag and made soothing noises. "No problem about our talking, though," she added hastily when Mike took a step toward the rack. "As long as you're here, you might as well go on with your questions."

His eyes narrowed as his gaze turned back to Charlie. "Boomer? Your cat?"

"No." She eyed the tote bag and prayed its occupant would give up and take a nap before all hell broke loose. After all, she'd bottle-fed Boomer only minutes before they'd left the house. He couldn't possibly be hungry again.

"Your dog?"

"No. That is, not exactly."

"Not exactly," Mike repeated slowly. The finely honed sixth sense that had never failed him demanded satisfaction. "Just what *do* you have in there?" He took another step toward the rack.

"A male baby wallaby, a type of kangaroo." Charlie blurted since she couldn't come up with another answer. "His name is Boomer. All male kangaroos are called Boomers."

Mike froze in midstride. "A male baby kangaroo? In here? I mean in there?" He pointed to the tote bag.

Charlie nodded and tried to act as if a kangaroo in an office was an everyday occurrence.

He ran his fingers through his hair in a gesture Charlie remembered all too well was a sign of his frustration. "Since when does the concierge of Blair House keep a kangaroo as a pet? Let alone carry it around with her like a baby?"

Charlie glowered at him. "Where is it written in my contract that I can't bring a pet into Blair House? Or that it has to be a cat or a dog?"

"Come on," Mike said, frustrated as hell. He knew that there was no such clause in her employment contract, but enough was enough. Not even an unusual woman like Charlie Norris would go to such weird lengths as to own a pet like a kangaroo. "You really don't expect me to believe a cockamamy story like that one, do you?"

She shrugged. "I'm beyond the point of trying to defend myself or my choice of pets to you or anyone else. Believe it or not, Boomer *is* a baby kangaroo and he needs five feedings a day. I bottle-fed him this morning before I came to work. Right now he thinks he's in his mother's pouch waiting for the next feeding."

At her explanation, Mike looked more incredulous than ever. "Why is he shaking like that?"

"He's just reacting to a friendly voice. Mine," she added pointedly.

Mike eyed the swaying tote bag. "Not that I believe you, but where did you manage to find a kangaroo around here? And why did you have to bring it to the office?"

"I found Boomer through the Internet. As for why he's here, Freddie, my zoo helper, has the flu. I didn't have anyone else to leave the little guy with."

"On the Internet. A zoo," Mike echoed slowly. "I've heard of Web sites where people sell or exchange all kinds of weird things, but baby kangaroos? And a personal zoo? You can't possibly be serious."

"He's here, isn't he? And, for your information, I own two other marsupials. They're my friends." She stopped and frowned. "Actually, I don't actually know who owns who, but collecting exotic animals is a hobby of mine."

Charlie wasn't sure she liked the rainbow of expressions that ran across Mike's face as he eyed the tote bag. If he'd thought she was odd before, what did he think of her now?

And why, she wondered as she eyed Mike's chiseled features and the aura of mystery that his profession surrounded him with, did she care what he thought of her?

"A zoo for exotic animals," he echoed softly as

he eyed her. "Now, why don't I believe that either?"

It was Charlie's turn to shrug. "It's a small zoo where I keep Boomer and his..." She paused for breath. What more could he think about her if she told him she had an eclectic collection of creatures, furry and otherwise? She settled for "...and a few other animals."

"And this so-called zoo of yours?" he said dryly. "Next thing you're going to tell me it's in your backyard."

"Exactly," she agreed, relieved that the cards were on the table. She could be herself again. "I have three acres of land in back of the house."

Mike was almost speechless. As far as he knew, kangaroos were regarded as pests by Australians, but evidently not by Charlie. But to carry around a baby kangaroo in a tote bag?

For Pete's sakes! Mike wanted to shout at her. This is Blair House, the official residence of the State Department! Numerous notables have stayed here through the years, including a president of the United States while the White House was being renovated. How could you bring a live kangaroo in here?

He glanced at the tote bag. On second thought, he didn't dare raise his voice. There was no telling how the baby kangaroo in there might react. What if it got out and he had to chase it around the premises? He and Charlie would be dismissed so fast it would make their heads swim. And what that would do to his spotless reputation wasn't even worth thinking about.

The terrifying thought changed the picture. He could look the other way, but he was the Special-Agent-in-Charge at Blair House, and had a duty to perform. If anything went wrong, it was his head.

Before she could stop him, Mike reached for the tote bag, pulled the strings open and looked inside.

Two big brown eyes looked trustfully back at him. A damp nose twitched, two little brownish-red elongated ears waved a welcome.

To add to Mike's dismay, a slender tongue licked its lips, a sure sign it was ready for its next bottle. To really blow his mind, he caught a glimpse of small hips encased in a diaper and a foot that was tapping to some unheard melody.

The little creature inside the tote bag *was* a baby kangaroo!

Mike could have sworn, if anyone had asked him later, that the animal had actually smiled at him.

What he did sense, was that he'd been foiled one more time by Charlie's unorthodox behavior and her mesmerizing eyes. Thank God, it was only a helpless baby kangaroo she had with her this time instead of something that could have caused a major incident.

He let the tote bag's drawstring close, muttered

under his breath and swung around to stare at the baby kangaroo's owner. When she smiled hopefully, words almost failed him.

"I can't deal with this right now," he muttered and dropped the sheaf of papers he was carrying on Charlie's desk.

The tote bag stopped shaking.

Charlie sighed in relief, put a warning finger over her lips and pointed to the door. "We can talk outside," she whispered.

"I can't believe you want to talk out in the hall because of your pet," Mike protested. "Why not here in your office? He can't possibly understand what we're talking about."

"I don't want to disturb Boomer," she whispered. "He needs his rest."

"You've got it wrong. He's not a baby. He's only a kangaroo!"

"Same thing." She grabbed him by the arm and urged him toward the door.

"No way! I'm not putting up with this," Mike said. He shook off her arm. "We'll talk another time when your pet isn't around."

Charlie unhappily watched Mike glare at the tote bag and head for the door. After this latest incident, there was no way she was ever going to be able to restore her credibility with him—if she had had any in the first place—or be able to change his opinion of her. At least, not until she had a chance to show

him how nearly human some of her pets actually
were. And had a chance to show him humans had a
lot to learn about relationships from the loving and
caring animals.

She turned back into her office and glanced
through the sheaf of papers Mike had dropped on
her desk. After a moment, she realized they were
copies of handwritten notes he'd taken about the incident yesterday. Several had question marks on the
side. Questions he'd obviously intended to ask her.

"Still don't trust me, do you?" she muttered as
she debated throwing the papers in the wastepaper
basket.

Mike unexpectedly appeared in the doorway.
"Maybe I was a little hasty back there," he said. "I
forgot to take my notes with me. Unless…" he went
on with a glance at the coatrack, "you've changed
your mind and want to go over them with me now."

Charlie glanced up at Mike. She could have
sworn her hormones snapped to attention and her
body start to tingle at his unexpected appearance.
After startling her out of a year's growth, he had a
lot of nerve trying to be friendly. Now, more than
ever, she was determined to show him how human
he could be if he tried. But with Boomer waiting
for his next feeding, she didn't dare take the time.
At full strength, Boomer sounded like a foghorn.
The last thing she needed was to attract any more
attention.

"No, thanks," she said with a smile. "As I said, I have a full schedule this morning. But leave the papers with me and I'll give them back to you later."

Mike started to turn away. "By the way," she called after him, "are you going to be at the employee picnic Sunday?"

"Picnic?"

Charlie fished in her desk drawer and handed him a handful of picnic flyers. "Try to make it. I think you're in for a pleasant surprise. And while you're at it, please leave a few copies in the butler's pantry on your way out."

Mike looked doubtful, but after another glance at the coatrack, folded the flyers and put them into his pocket. "As usual, you're not making much sense," he muttered. "But if you want to play games, I'm willing to give it a try." He glanced at Charlie as if he wanted to say something more before he shook his head and left.

With a rueful glance at the quiet tote bag, Charlie dropped into the chair behind her desk. Boomer could wait for his next feeding until she had a chance to come up with the answers to the question marks on Mike's list. When she returned the papers, Mike would have to admit that the only thing she'd been guilty of yesterday was trying to do her job. And of being in the wrong place at the wrong time.

As for Boomer and the rest of the zoo population

she planned on introducing Mike to, she was positive that once he met them in a more natural setting their personalities were bound to hook him for sure. Just as Boomer had captured her heart the first time she'd seen his picture on the Internet and found out that he was for sale.

If Boomer and the rest of his animal friends didn't manage to humanize Mike, nothing could.

FRIDAYS HAD NEVER been a particularly good day, Mike mused as he strode along the corridor away from Charlie's office. The only good thing about this one was that it brought the end of the week. After midnight tonight he had two peaceful days off to look forward to, thank God.

Two days without Charlie Norris and her cute but bizarre pet. He muttered his displeasure under his breath as he strode across the marble floor to his office and, at the same time, tried to rub the kink out of the back of his neck. As far back as he could recall, the only time that damn kink showed up was when he was under stress. No big surprise it showed up this time. He could lay the credit for this episode on Charlie Norris and that baby kangaroo of hers. Bottle-feeding! Diapers! Hell, you'd think that Blair House was an animal nursery instead of a prestigious home away from home for VIPs.

"Wheeler! Wait up!"

Mike stopped in midstride and turned around. His

superior, Bradley Simons, beckoned him into his office and closed the door behind them.

"Have a seat." Simons walked around his desk and dropped into his chair. "Got a job for you."

"I've already got a job," Mike answered.

"Well, now you've got another one." Simons reached into his desk drawer for a bottle of pills. "Hand me that pitcher over there, please." He shook out two large pills, put them in his mouth and washed them down with water. "Sorry, with all the crap going on, that ulcer of mine is acting up again. Guess it comes with the territory."

Mike rubbed the back of his head when the thought of Charlie and her pet began to show all the signs of turning into a headache and a half. "Tell me about it."

Simons eyed him sympathetically. "You, too?"

Mike shrugged. "Like you said, it comes with the territory."

"Glad you feel that way." Simons rummaged in his center desk drawer, took out two letters and handed them across the desk. "Take a look at those."

Mike read the first letter. His lips set in a grim line as he read the second. Both letters threatened the Blair House personnel for their interference in the attempted assassination yesterday. "Kind of soon for these to show up."

Simons leaned back in his chair. "Make a guy

angry enough…'' His voice trailed off. ''You notice that the author keeps referring to our Charlie Norris?''

Mike had noticed, all right, but he hadn't thought of the lady as being ''our'' Charlie. Maybe she was Simons's Charlie, but not his. Not after the way the pain was growing at the back of his neck and threatening to take his head off. She may have pleaded her innocence when he'd confronted her after the shooting, but it looked as if she had managed to annoy the hell out of someone out there. ''What was she supposed to do, let the two jackasses kill each other?''

Simons shrugged. ''Right or wrong, she's a target. I want you to keep an eye on her.''

Mike blinked. Of all the assignments he could have drawn, guarding Charlie wasn't at the top of his list. ''Don't tell me that that's the new job!''

''Yep.'' Simons stood. ''Get used to it.'' He gestured to a picnic flyer Mike had sticking out of his breast pocket. ''You can start with the picnic.''

Mike got to his feet and bit back a protest. ''I hadn't made up my mind to go to the picnic, sir.''

''Sure you have,'' Simons said amiably as he opened the office door. ''Enjoy the day.''

Chapter Three

At midmorning Sunday, Mike checked the address on the picnic flyer against the address on the little red barn mailbox. They were one and the same. The empty field across the road was filled with automobiles, SUVs and motorcycles.

It looked as if Charlie *had* offered her property for the annual Blair House picnic. That seemed normal enough, but what really got to him was the lack of security personnel at the gate.

He bit his lower lip. With Charlie Norris in charge, he was almost afraid to think of the surprise she said she had in store for him.

What bothered him even more than the lack of security was the conventional, rambling yellow-and-white Cape Cod-style farmhouse. Surrounded by trees and flowering azalea bushes, and with beds of peonies and day lilies randomly placed to make them look as if they grew there naturally, it wasn't the type of setting he'd expected the unconventional Charlie to own.

On second thought, he wasn't sure *what* type of house he'd expected Charlie to live in, but this traditional cottage sure wasn't it. After she'd told him she had a zoo in her backyard, he'd almost expected her to live in a wooden cabin set in a stand of trees surrounded by animal cages.

"Daddy, hurry." A small hand tugged at Mike's knee and pointed to the balloon-decorated side gate. "Hurry up before all the balloons are gone!"

Mike tore his gaze away from the house and moved on.

Mob scenes weren't his idea of entertainment, he mused as he followed the red arrows that pointed to the side gate. It was the idea of any open gathering in unguarded settings that made him uneasy.

He'd been trained to be wary of open spaces where he couldn't control the setting or protect his charges.

This one really disturbed him. Bringing his son Jake along didn't sit well with him, but he'd tentatively promised him they would come to the picnic before Simons had given him his new assignment. He'd had no choice.

With Jake's little hand in his, Mike made his way around to the back of the property. Accustomed to checking every detail of his surroundings, he mentally counted twenty-eight women in shorts and

T-shirts decorated with a Blair House logo. True to form, thirty-two men in jogging shorts or jeans and the same Blair House T-shirts were gathered in small groups and drinking beer.

The children were more difficult to account for. They never seemed to stand in one place long enough to count heads, anyway.

The casual T-shirts had to be a management give-away because everyone wore them, even the kids. From a security viewpoint, in his opinion, they were the last item of clothing they should all have been wearing. If a problem arose, with every kid wearing the same T-shirt it would be difficult to tell one from another. As for putting a T-shirt on Jake or himself, no way. It wasn't only foolhardy, the word *casual* wasn't in his vocabulary.

Picnics weren't exactly his style, Mike mused as he continued to check out the surroundings while deciding whether to remain or leave. But, he reminded himself, he was not only here on orders, there was Jake, a thirty-seven-inch-tall, three-and-a-half-year-old bundle of energy to consider.

Then, too, he'd been promising himself he'd take up a normal life again, and, after a year of promises, he reluctantly figured it was about time to begin. Not for his sake—with a leg still aching from a bullet he'd taken during an attempted assassination, he could have done without picnics—but because of Jake.

As a single parent, he owed the kid big.

He smiled fondly at his son. "What color?"

"Green," Jake said firmly. A frown crossed his little forehead. "No, red. I want a red one."

"Cool, sport," Mike agreed with a covert glance around the territory. So far, so good. "Let's go and see if we can get you one of each."

This shouldn't be a problem, Mike told himself as they made their way across the wide expanse of grass to where a clown was blowing up balloons. The bigger problem facing him was how to make up to Jake for the loss of his mother in a boating accident a year ago.

As for seeing many familiar faces at the picnic, he hadn't been assigned to Blair House on a regular basis long enough to have cultivated any real friendships. Except perhaps Charlie Norris. Now that he thought about their recent exchange over her odd choice of pets, he wasn't sure Charlie fitted into the friendship category. Or, better yet, he thought as his imagination suddenly took flight, into his arms.

He'd never known anyone like Charlie Norris, he thought as they strolled around the grounds checking out the activity. The bigger surprise was that his attraction to her had turned into something beyond fascination before he'd realized what had hit him. Considering that business and pleasure didn't mix, any ideas along that line had to stop. Especially since she had become his official charge.

He simply couldn't afford to let his interest in her go any further.

He gazed casually around the picnic grounds as they made their way to the clown. On the surface, everything looked harmless, but he wasn't prepared to relax his vigilance. On one hand, there had been Charlie's involvement in the love affair between Wade Stevens and the Baronovian duchess. Then there was the recent shooting in Blair House. There were too many unusual happenings that Charlie had managed to become involved with. He needed to stay on his toes if he was going to keep her alive.

Granted, Charlie had always claimed good intentions, but as far as he was concerned it had only been by the grace of God that neither she nor anyone else had gotten killed by now. Between his reaction to those unhappy incidents and the incongruous encounter with her pet kangaroo, he didn't expect many friendly words from her today. How to stay on a friendly footing and keep from blowing their tenuous relationship was priority number one.

"Daddy," Jake said. "I'm hungry."

"Me too, sport. Let's go see what we can find." Mike took a fresh look around him for any food vendors. With one balloon tied to Jake's wrist and the other carefully tied to the shoulder strap of his little denim overalls, they set off to explore the picnic area. It was soon clear that it was a case of finding something for Jake to eat or having to leave, which he couldn't possibly do and still keep an eye on Charlie.

Picnics were usually catered, but not this one. Too late, he remembered that the flyer had said this was a do-it-yourself picnic. Damn! True to form, Charlie's picnic had to be different. He sighed as he gazed over at a group of women laying out home-made fried chicken and potato salad on picnic tables, and at the men busy at portable barbecues.

He sobered as the setting began to remind him of a long-ago picnic he'd attended with his new bride before Jake had been born. Ellie had been annoyed by the rustic surroundings and lack of what she thought of as comfort. He hadn't dwelt on the possibilities of picnics since.

One thought led to another, and he was reminded of something he hadn't wanted to think of.

It had been a year since he'd forced himself to put the past and his late wife's accidental drowning behind him. Longer, if he counted the months from the time Ellie had decided to relive her carefree youth, free from husband and child, a decision that had left him without a wife and Jake without a mother.

What had made him think now of Ellie and the role she could have played in his and Jake's life beat the hell out of him. Maybe he hadn't done as good a job of putting the past behind him as he thought he had.

It certainly couldn't have been the sight of Charlie Norris staking out a position under an apple tree. Or could it?

For a moment, he hadn't recognized her without the tailored suit she usually wore on duty. In her brief cream-colored shorts and that damn T-shirt that seemed to be today's dress code she made his testosterone jump to attention.

Her T-shirt revealed more of Charlie's slender and curvaceous figure than it was intended to conceal. Considering the state of their friendship, or the lack of it, it was strange that the idea of her wearing that skimpy outfit for everyone within shouting distance bothered him. Even the idea that he was bothered annoyed him.

The sight of Charlie in her too-tight T-shirt and the wicked smile she exchanged with the male picnickers came close to driving him out of his mind. Considering that their relationship was a hands-off situation, he was forced to chalk up another reason to stay at least ten feet away from the lady. He was jealous!

In his frustration, he ran his hand across his forehead. When had his fascination for her unorthodox behavior turned into a grudging but growing attraction? And where in the hell was it going to get him in the long run, anyway?

He took Jake's hand and started toward a large, wooded fenced-off area that surely housed Charlie's zoo. At least the animals would take Jake's mind off lunch. A meat-and-potato man himself, he wistfully wished for a hamburger. Not the best of choices for Jake, but he doubted anyone would be offering Jake's current choice of food; peanut butter and jelly sandwiches.

His stomach growled. Thank God he had his mother to help keep an eye on Jake and to feed him during the week. If it had been left up to him, the kid would have lived on fast food hamburgers and French fried potatoes. Unfortunately, his mother, who would have known to bring food to a do-it-yourself picnic, was off visiting a close friend for a few days. Thus the care and feeding of Jake this weekend was up to him. Unfortunately, he didn't seem to be doing a good job of it.

"Daddy! Daddy!" Jake hollered as he jumped up and down and pointed to the sky. The red balloon Mike had tied to Jake's wrist had broken loose and was slowly floating away in the breeze. Before he could stop him, Jake ran after the balloon with Mike hard at his heels shouting for him to wait up.

The breeze grew stronger. The balloon picked up speed and sailed straight toward where Charlie was unpacking a picnic basket. To Mike's surprise, she leapt to her feet and managed to catch the balloon before it sailed over her head.

Jake crowed happily and, before Mike could grab him, made a mad dash for the balloon—and Charlie.

Charlie laughed when a little boy ran into her and grabbed her around her knees. Amused, she handed him the errant balloon and, to her delight, was rewarded by a kiss and a hug.

Her smile faded when Mike Wheeler skidded to a stop in front of her.

"Thanks," Mike said as he retied the balloon to Jake's wrist. "I'm afraid I wouldn't have caught it in time."

Charlie's eyes widened as she glanced down at the laughing little boy. To her surprise, he was a miniature duplicate of Mike, complete with golden-brown hair, blue eyes and a child-sized killer smile.

"Yours?"

"Mine. His name is Jake." He looked down at the little boy. "Jake, this is Miss Charlie Norris. How about thanking her for saving your balloon?"

Wheels began to turn in Charlie's head. Had Mike ever mentioned he was married? Or that he had a child? For that matter, when had he ever said anything about his private life? Never. So where did the kid come in?

She searched over Mike's shoulder. "Where's your wife?"

"She died a year ago," he answered, his hands on Jake's shoulders to keep him from darting away again. "There's just me and Jake."

"I'm sorry," she said, itching to know what had happened to the late Mrs. Wheeler but too embarrassed to ask. The tight look around Mike's eyes would have stopped her, anyway. She'd already guessed he was a man who kept his off-duty life private.

"Thanks again for your help," Mike repeated. He took his son's hand in his and started off across the lawn.

Charlie nodded and headed back to her blanket. Regardless of having worked in close proximity to Mike Wheeler at Blair House for the past year, she didn't know him any better than he knew her.

Looking back over her shoulder, she saw the ever-watchful Mike lounging against an apple tree with his hands across his chest, never taking his eyes off Jake who'd stopped to investigate a rock. The expression on his face and the soft look in his eyes as he gazed at the boy told her how much the boy meant to him. She found herself smiling. Contrary to her earlier impression, maybe Mike *was* a man with a heart.

Gone were the traditional Secret Service black suit, white shirt and black tie that enabled him to fade into a background. In khaki slacks and jacket, a gray polo shirt and casual leather loafers, he looked like a new and different man. If the old one had attracted her, this new one had her full attention. He certainly didn't resemble the all-business man he'd appeared to be ever since they'd first met. Today she was seeing a side of him he seldom showed to anyone.

Judging from the way he behaved with his son, Mike Wheeler was strong on the outside yet tender beneath the surface. He could be protective and nurturing, she thought as she gazed at him. But not with her.

To her secret regret, almost every man she met treated her like a sister or a friend. They even laughed at her carefree attitude and the oddball ideas she came up with.

Most of the men she met never saw her as a desirable woman.

The look in Mike's eyes when he thought she wasn't noticing told her that, in spite of himself, he thought she was hot. And, to her growing surprise, his interest made her feel womanly.

The long and the short of it was that, even though she was thirty-five and had successfully established her independence years ago, Mike made her yearn for someone of her own to watch over her.

But Mike by profession was a lawman. She had vowed never to fall for a lawman and, like her own mother, take the chance that someday she would have her heart broken.

"Daddy!" Jake ran back to his father. "I'm still hungry!"

Charlie heard Jake complain. It didn't look as if Mike had brought lunch with him. She bit her lip, made up her mind to put her musings aside and went to join him. It was only a friendly gesture she had in mind. What could happen? "Can I help?"

"I'm afraid I didn't think to bring anything for lunch," Mike said with a helpless shrug. "I guess I thought I'd find a food vendor here. I'll have to take Jake back into town."

"But Daddy, there's the zoo!"

Mike tried to connect a zoo with lunch and came up empty. "What about the zoo?"

"You said there's a zoo here, Daddy."

Charlie rushed to explain. "I was planning on taking anyone who's interested to visit my zoo later this afternoon. The animals aren't as frisky as they are in the morning."

Jake's eyes lit up. "I want to go to the zoo now!"

Mike held Jake by an arm before he could start off by himself again. "You actually have a zoo of your own?"

Charlie looked offended. "You still didn't believe me?"

Left unsaid was the implication he should have known she was telling the truth. Even if the truth in this case was something most people would never have believed anyway. But then, Charlie wasn't most people.

"Right," he answered dryly. "Face it. A zoo isn't the sort of thing most people have in their backyard."

Charlie silently gestured to the mutinous expression on Jake's face. "Now that you're here, it would be a shame to miss the tour."

"Guess so," Mike muttered. "But if there's a choice between the zoo and Jake's lunch…"

"How about a hamburger and some veggies?" She pointed to the picnic basket. "I have enough for all of us."

"Jake?"

"No peanut and jelly sandwiches?"

"No, I'm sorry." Charlie answered with a proper sad look on her face. "But I do have celery sticks filled with peanut butter."

"Cool!" Jake grinned happily.

Charlie grinned back. Anything with peanut butter was obviously okay with him.

Mike took the plunge. "If your offer includes me, I'll take the hamburger."

Charlie hesitated, debating whether she should tell Mike the truth before he found it out for himself— the hard way. She couldn't fib—she'd said hamburgers, but the truth was something different.

She rummaged in the picnic basket, found the celery-and-peanut-butter sticks wrapped in a plastic bag and handed them to Jake. With a calculating glance at Mike, she took out two round bundles wrapped in foil and handed him one. "I think I should warn you this is a different kind of hamburger."

Mike unwrapped the foil bundle and stared at

the green and brown contents. "It sure looks different. Is it really a hamburger?"

"It's made from tofu and vegetables. I love animals too much to eat meat," she added, looking horrified at the thought.

Mike grimaced. "No meat?"

"No."

Mike hid his trepidation. Of course, a lover and collector of kangaroos and the Lord knew what else would never eat meat. He was afraid to ask if she had any chickens in that zoo of hers.

Since she was feeding Jake, eating a veggie burger without comment seemed to be the least he could do.

"Sure," he said bravely. "May I pay you?"

Charlie frowned. "I thought this was a favor between friends!"

Mike hid a smile. Friendly. He was making some progress after all, but knowing Charlie, he wasn't quite sure how much and in which direction—good or bad. "Er…okay. The next favor is on me."

Ten minutes later, Charlie caught sight of Mike covertly rolling up the remains of the veggie burger in its foil wrapping. She hid a smile. She was willing to bet that after a visit to her zoo where he'd meet her pets, Mike wouldn't order meat for a while either.

Mike gazed around the grounds. Women were packing the picnic baskets, younger children were on the verge of falling sleep, older children were playing games and the men were still drinking beer. "You haven't taken any security precautions, have you?"

"No. Why would I?" Charlie asked. Mike was obviously back to looking at everything as though it were a threat. "This is my home and these people are friends."

"Maybe so," he replied. "But the fact remains you've invited a hundred people to visit you without a security check. To top it off, you have a zoo full of exotic animals that are probably worth good money. In my book, those are damn good reasons for having some kind of security precautions."

With Mike reverting to the all-business persona who saw danger everywhere, Charlie's pleasure cooled. "Don't you ever let yourself relax?"

For a moment he looked surprised. "Not when it counts."

"Ridiculous. I told you, most of these people are my friends."

"Heck," he answered as he searched the area for Jake, "with everyone wearing the same T-shirts, they all look alike. You've given anyone who doesn't belong here a perfect cover."

He covered his eyes with a hand and squinted into the sun.

"Looking for suspects?" Charlie covered the

picnic basket with a small cotton towel and got to her feet.

"No. At the moment, I'm looking for Jake. See the green balloon moving over there? That's Jake. I tied the balloon to his overalls. Best security idea I ever thought of," he added with a satisfied grin.

Charlie swallowed a tart remark. Maybe Mike was human, after all.

"When does this tour of yours begin?" Mike asked. "I'd like to get Jake home before he falls asleep on his feet."

"I was going to do the tour first," Charlie said after a thoughtful glance around. "But maybe I'll wait until after wc havc a few games."

"That'll wake everyone up, for sure," he said dryly. "Are you really the only hostess of this shindig?"

"Mostly." She took a whistle out of her pocket. "Kids' games first, then it will be the grown-ups' chance."

"To make fools out of ourselves?"

"Don't knock it, Mr. Wheeler," she said with a sassy smile. "If you lightened up a little, you might even have some fun like a normal human being."

Mike gazed after Charlie as she walked to the middle of the grassy area. He couldn't help admiring her swaying hips, the inviting smile that lit up her face when she glanced back at him over her shoulder and the way her silken hair blew across her shoulders in the afternoon breeze.

Charlie was wrong about him, he thought as he smothered a smile. He was not only human, he was beginning to feel more normal by the minute.

Charlie was a handful, but it was her innate sensuality and the way that damned T-shirt strained against her breasts that made his body warm and his thoughts turn to subjects best left unexplored.

The attraction wasn't only physical, he admitted wryly. To give the lady credit, there was her intelligence, her wry sense of humor and the unlikely way she managed to march to her own private drummer and still come up smelling like a rose that made him want to get closer to her.

What he didn't approve of was the side of her personality that put her squarely in the middle of any trouble that came along. And he hated the way she managed to get him mixed up with her in her latest disaster.

Whoever the real Charlie Norris was, she was an intriguing bundle of womanhood that any red-blooded man could appreciate. Except that he had no room in his life right now for anyone but Jake.

Becoming involved with a woman, Charlie Norris in particular, would definitely be a mistake.

A voice came over a loudspeaker. "Attention, everyone! Attention! We're about to start the mother-and-son relay races. Mothers, get ready!"

Mike watched as the balloon attached to Jake floated back over in Charlie's direction. He smiled fondly and started to follow his son. It wasn't strange the kid was attracted to Charlie. She had the kind of warmth and vitality that kids instinctively were drawn to.

He reached Charlie just as Jake slid to a halt in front of her. And was just in time to hear the words that made his head spin and the bottom drop out of his world.

''Miss Charlie, everybody here gots a mommy except me. Would you please be my mommy so I can race, too?''

Chapter Four

Mike's smile faded. Of all the words his mind and certainly his heart weren't ready for, it was *mommy*. Charlie Norris, of all people! The last woman who would fit the bill!

That was going too far and too fast, he thought as he ran his fingers through his hair and tried to put the smile back on his face. Oh, Charlie was attractive enough, he'd give her that. Smart, too. Maybe too smart for her own good. But maternal? Hell, he thought as he gazed at her over Jake's head, of all the words that he could have used to describe Charlie, *maternal* wasn't on the list. She was too flighty to be a responsible parent.

Except maybe when it came to that kangaroo she'd treated like a baby. As far as he was concerned, mothering an animal, no matter how admirable, didn't count.

"Sorry about that," he muttered. "I don't have

the slightest notion where that came from." He put his hands on Jake's shoulders.

With a quick shake of her head, she put out a hand to stay him. "Don't worry, Mike. I understand. He's only a little boy. Kids usually say what they think one minute and forget it the next. Besides," she added with a grin, "I'll only be his mother just long enough for the race."

Charlie tried to hide her reaction to the look of panic that passed over Mike's eyes. The way his clear blue eyes turned a deep gray spoke louder than anything he could have said. He obviously regarded her as the last woman he would care to have for Jake's substitute mother.

She decided to let the incident pass. Being asked to play mommy may have given her a twinge or two, but she had the picnic to see to and a life of her own afterwards to enjoy.

She smoothed the little boy's unruly hair away from his face. "You're on, Jake, if it's okay with your father," she said, gazing at the virile man who often occupied her thoughts. Of all people to be Jake's father! Why was the man she was attracted to so clearly not the man for her?

"I wanna go with Miss Charlie now," Jake said stubbornly. He grabbed Charlie's hand and tried to pull her along with him. "Bye, Daddy."

Mike knew when he was licked. He let go of Jake's shoulders. "Come right back when the race is over.'' Too late. Jake and his temporary mother were already on their way.

He watched the two head for Charlie's picnic blanket to pick up the batons for use in the relay race. Sure enough, she was quietly talking to Jake who, to Mike's surprise, was listening intently and nodding his head. Whatever she was saying, it looked as if Jake was eating it up.

It sure couldn't have been the celery-and-peanut-butter sticks Charlie had given Jake for lunch that had won the kid over, no way. Or the way she'd agreed to pretend to be his mother for the race. It had to be something more. Maybe Jake saw something in Charlie that only a child could see.

''You must have bribed him with the promise of a peanut butter and jelly sandwich!'' Mike called, eyeing his antsy son as they walked by him on their way to the starting line. ''I'll have to remember to do that for future use.''

''No bribe,'' Charlie smiled. ''I just explained we have something important to think about right now. Like winning the race. He can't wait.'' She paused to shake her head at Jake who was back to pulling at her hand. ''He obviously isn't into delayed gratification, is he?''

Mike had to agree. Delayed gratification was a hard enough concept for a grown man to understand; he was still grappling with it himself. And that included considering a possible affair with, of all women, Charlie.

Damn, he thought as he watched Charlie and Jake take their places at the starting line. The lady had to be smarter than he'd thought or she wouldn't always manage to stay one step ahead of him so easily.

He eyed her skintight T-shirt, the cream shorts that barely covered critical parts of her anatomy and her long, slim legs as she jogged across the lawn. With a slender waist, those appealing legs and a body he would have loved to explore, she was clearly in a class by herself. She was, if he had his head screwed on right, a woman to avoid.

There was no doubt about it, his mind and his body weren't going down the same track.

Nonsense, considering the way Charlie's laid-back personality usually made him grit his teeth. He'd planned to leave as soon as the race was over, but he realized now he couldn't do it. Not now, not here and not yet.

He was startled out of his puzzled reverie by the sharp, unmistakable sound of a starter's pistol going off. A pistol, after he'd warned Charlie about the lack of security on the premises! Why couldn't she use a whistle like any sane person?

He muttered every cussword he'd ever learned during his varied career, some of which he didn't even understand, and started toward the race location at double time.

How in the hell did Charlie manage to keep coming up with the ideas that made his pragmatic mind blanch?

She'd overlooked hiring guards to screen the picnic guests.

She'd allowed the picnic attendees to wear identical T-shirts so that they all wound up looking alike.

Now, she'd actually allowed a starter's pistol on the premises!

In his book, Charlie had managed to violate every security rule for public gatherings. She also took the cake for being irresponsible. In the process, she'd put his guts in a knot one more time.

Didn't she realize there were crazies everywhere? he muttered as he ran through the cheering crowd. Hadn't she been listening to him when he'd explained the need for security? Especially when most of the guests had to be government employees who attracted trouble like flies?

Hadn't she learned anything from her experience at the shooting last week at Blair House?

A fine sheen of fear covered his forehead. A hard lump clogged his throat. He picked up speed and promised himself that when he caught up with Charlie, he'd wring her pretty neck.

He reached the halfway point in the race in time to see Jake cross the finish line and hand his baton to Charlie. Before he had a chance to get her attention, she grabbed the baton out of Jake's hands and raced back up the slope as if a wind was at her sneaker-clad heels.

Mike swore and headed back to the starting line where the race had started and where it would end. She didn't know it yet, but he planned on being there when she reached it. No way was the lady going to get away without listening to another—and this time, more emphatic—lesson on the need for security!

She was going to have to understand taking security precautions had to be number one on her priority list on and off her job. Number two, any type of gun was a no-no. Especially when she had his son in her custody.

Pumped up with his mission, he raced around the perimeter of the crowed. To his dismay, he reached the finish just in time to realize that if Charlie kept up the path she'd taken she was bound to collide with him.

Instinctively, Mike braced himself and opened his arms to catch her.

Charlie hit Mike's chest hard enough to knock him down and take her with him. She put her arms around his neck, held on tight and, laughing helplessly, gazed down into his eyes. What she saw reflected there made her swallow her laughter.

This was just a harmless, unexpected embrace, an accident, wasn't it? she asked herself as she stared into his blue eyes. So why did Mike look as if he'd never seen her before now?

"We won!" she said breathlessly and gave him a congratulatory kiss on his lips. Pulling back, she was surprised by the change that came over him.

"Sorry about that." She eyed the deep, warm expression in his eyes and suddenly found she didn't feel sorry. Not a bit. She not only liked being in his arms, but the changes in his body were getting more interesting by the moment. Instead of being angry, Mike was apparently turned on by her!

She'd have to think about this if she ever had a minute to herself.

Seconds later, she realized she was not only lying on top of him, he was holding her longer than he needed to. She felt the rapid beat of his heart, saw his eyes sharpen as he gazed at her. Her body reacted in ways no lady's should—at least not in public.

It wasn't just the race and Mike's reaction that took her breath away, Charlie realized as she waited for her heart to settle down into its normal beat. It was more than that; it was her own unexpected sensual response to the warmth of his lips and to the strength of the muscular arms that held her.

Most of all, it was her bewilderment at the powerful look of desire that had passed over his face so quickly she couldn't be sure she'd really seen it. For a split second, he'd actually looked as if he was about to kiss her back!

She had to be wrong. Knowing Mike and the way he kept scolding her for what he felt was her unorthodox behavior, she couldn't even be sure the sensuous look had ever been there at all.

Hoots, whistles and sexual innuendoes filled the air. To her chagrin, their audience cheered. Someone shouted, ''You go girl!'' She wanted to fade into the landscape. How would she be able to face anyone tomorrow with a straight face? Including Mike?

Fat chance of disappearing into the landscape when the man who was holding her was as handsome and as sexy as Mike Wheeler. Because of the nature of his profession, this man had an aura of mystery about him that women found irresistible. She was all too aware that almost every woman watching would have loved to trade places with her.

She swallowed hard at the thought. As far as she was concerned, they were welcome to him. Only later, not just yet. Not before she had a chance to find out why Mike had looked as if he'd wanted to hold her in his arms forever.

She kept a teasing smile on her face and gently started to wiggle out of his embrace. ''You can let me go now, you know, I really wasn't going to fall. It was only because you grabbed me,'' she said with a quick glance around. ''What will everyone think?''

"I never thought you were going to," Mike answered. "As to what people might think, I don't give a damn." He dropped his arms away from the soft warmth of her body, struggled to his feet and reached down to help her up. "Sorry..." he started to say, then stopped short. In his book, he had nothing to apologize for. It had been an accident, pure and simple.

On the other hand, while he wasn't going to admit it, what he obviously needed was to have his head examined for holding on to Charlie in the first place. With or without an audience.

"Then why did you bother to catch me?"

"Damned if I know," he answered as he shook his head to clear it. "Maybe I've been out in the sun too long."

Mike felt like a fool. Why *had* he caught and held on to her? More to the point, how could he explain the urge to kiss her? How could he explain that if he had given in to the urge to really kiss her, he wouldn't have been able to stop with one kiss?

He was an ass even to think about it!

This *was* Charlie Norris, the woman who drove him crazy, wasn't it? The woman he'd vowed to keep at a safe distance while he tried to save her from herself?

Even as he denied knowing why he'd held Charlie in his arms long past the need to keep her safe, he knew the truth: he'd wanted to hold Charlie in his arms for months. First to shake her to get her attention, then to kiss her senseless.

Gazing into her eyes, he wasn't really sure he knew which road to take. All he could remember was that he'd wanted to hold her and kiss her from the time she'd knocked him down at the royal wedding at Baronovia.

He gazed at Charlie in wonderment. Now that he held her by her suntanned arms she felt softer—and somehow smelled sweeter than before.

As for that kiss... Against all logic, after gazing into Charlie's molten-blue eyes, the kiss was beginning to sound like a darn good idea.

"You're a problem, you know that, don't you?" he said as he gazed into the teasing eyes that managed to disturb him so.

"Who, me?"

"Yes, you. Beginning with the Baronovia caper and to today's use of a starter's pistol, you never seem to think or operate logically." He didn't add that he was more annoyed with himself for even considering kissing her than he was at her lack of good sense.

He swallowed hard. If he kept up thinking along these lines, he'd wind up compromising the all-business code by which he lived. Not even Jake's late mother had had this effect on him.

A voice came over the bullhorn and saved him from hearing Charlie's answer.

"Okay, folks. Now that the ladies have had their chance, how about a dad-and-daughter relay race?"

Mike dropped his arms. If he'd had a daughter, he would have welcomed the opportunity to break away from Charlie. As it was, he'd have to settle for feeling like a jerk and hoping she didn't realize how close he'd come to making a fool of himself.

Falling for Charlie was out, he told himself one more time. He knew from experience he would wind up feeling like an idiot.

"Excuse me for a minute," Charlie said when someone called to her. "I have something to take care of." She disappeared into the crowd.

He looked around for Jake. Damn, where was the kid when he needed him? He intended to tell him they'd stick around only until after the zoo tour. For Jake's sake, he told himself. If he'd been alone, he would have run for the nearest exit before she came up with some other harebrained idea.

Women like Charlie were dangerous to a man's sanity, he thought grimly as he searched for the balloon he'd attached to Jake. Intentionally or not, they had a way of playing on a man's good nature until he couldn't think straight.

"Okay, all you husbands and significant others!" A voice shouted over the bullhorn. "Grab your partner and get ready for the three-legged race!"

Mike sighed with relief. He was home free. He was no one's husband or significant other. As for picnics, or any other celebrations, he should have learned his lesson. Events, especially if planned by Charlie Norris, were out. Although he had to admit she was soft, sweet-smelling and, in spite of her foibles, utterly feminine.

He'd reckoned without Jake. No sooner had the announcement of the three-legged race faded away, than he heard his son's enthusiastic voice beside him.

"Daddy! It's your turn now!"

"I don't think so," Mike said firmly. "We're leaving. I don't have a partner and, even if I did, I'm not going to put my leg to a test."

"Which leg is that?" Charlie asked innocently as she rejoined him. "I forgot."

"The left one," Mike answered automatically before he realized he'd laid himself open to Charlie's maneuvering. Maybe she'd gotten the wrong idea about him when he'd caught her. Maybe he should have shown a little less interest when he had his arms around her. "That is…"

"Then there's no problem," she broke in with a sidelong glance at Mike's leg. "Your father can use his right leg. I'll use my left."

To Mike's amusement, Jake looked bewildered and glanced down at his own short legs. From the expression on his son's face, Mike wasn't sure the kid knew the difference between the left and right leg, and he sure wasn't able to envision his father and Charlie tied together and hopping toward a finish line.

Besides, he reassured himself with a thoughtful glance at his son, the kid had to know even less about matchmaking.

Mike turned his attention to Charlie. She looked as cute and innocent as hell, but something about the look in her eyes told him he was being set up. ''Your doing?''

''Who, me?'' Her eyes widened, a smile lurked at the corner of her lips. ''You may not know it, Mr. Wheeler, but we always have a three-legged race at our picnics. Sack races, too.''

Tongue in cheek, Charlie waited while Mike thought it over—to race or not to race. From the expressions that crossed his face, it was evident she was driving him crazy. She didn't care. She wasn't looking for any kind of relationship with him, short of a business one, that is. What she did want was to humanize the man, make him realize no one was perfect. She wanted to have him stop pointing out her shortcomings when it was obvious to her he had a few of his own.

Shortcomings! The word really turned her off. She might not see her job at Blair House in the same way Mike did, but she always managed to get the job done, didn't she? What was wrong with getting it done in her own style and in her own way?

Even if it meant having Boomer, her pet baby

kangaroo, hanging from her office coatrack while she baby-sat the little darling.

Maybe it was the nature of his profession, but Mike took himself and everything he encountered too seriously. He seldom smiled, but she had to admit that when he did his smile turned her bones to jelly. Too bad he didn't smile more often.

"Come on, Mike," she coaxed. "You don't have a real excuse for not participating in the race. If you're afraid your leg will bother you, I'll even let you lean on me for support."

Excited by the idea, Jake jumped up and down. "Do it, Daddy! It's your turn."

"Why?" Mike asked. The last thing he wanted was to lean on Charlie, or to make a greater fool of himself than he already had.

Jake waved a blue ribbon. "Because Miss Charlie and I won this in the relay race. It's your turn to win a ribbon, too."

Mike gave in. He had to. His manhood had been challenged in front of Charlie. "There's no guarantee we'll win, son."

"You will if you have Miss Charlie for your partner. She's lots of fun!"

Mike didn't even want to think about being so close to Charlie. He gave in when he saw a challenging smile on his prospective partner's face. "Okay," he said, attempting to give in with good grace. Maybe three-legged races were the norm at picnics. It was the idea of being closely tied to Charlie that made him feel uncomfortable. "It had better be time for the zoo tour pretty soon," he muttered under his breath. "I don't know how much more of this 'fun' I can take."

Jake whooped. "I'll go get the rope!"

With Mike's trouser leg wound up to his right knee and his good leg loosely tied to Charlie's left leg, they lined up with the other contestants. As far as he was concerned, Charlie's skin felt too soft and too warm for comfort and definitely took his concentration off the race. The soft sigh she gave when they were instructed to put their arms around each other while their legs were bound together was sensuous as hell and did nothing to cool his already awakened body.

If mere physical contact with Charlie was able to do this to him, Mike knew he was in deep trouble. He was tempted to run, not walk, to the end of the race, to head for home as fast as his car could take him before she came up with some other idea bound to make him look foolish.

"Ready?" To Mike's discomfiture, the man in charge of the starting gun pointed it in the air and started to count. "One, two and three! Go!" The pistol went off.

Charlie took a firm grip on his shoulder. On the count of three, she was off like an arrow, dragging him with her. He swore under his breath and zeroed his attention in on the finish line. The damn thing looked as if it were at least a mile away.

With Mike holding on to her for dear life, her leg warm from rubbing against his, it was all Charlie could do to concentrate on the race. Maybe warm flesh on warm flesh hadn't been the best idea she could have come up with.

"Are you sure you're okay with this?" she asked Mike.

"A hell of a time to ask," he answered between gasps of pain.

The arm that had held her so tightly to him began to slip off her shoulder. Four steps later, his footsteps faltered. The rope that loosely bound them together began to slip. When his bare leg tangled with hers, the friction ignited an electric current that ran up her leg and to points north.

"This should help," she said when Mike began to mutter under his breath. He sounded so miserable her conscience began to bother her. She realized maybe this was neither the time nor the place to try to humanize the man. "Try to follow me. If we coordinate this, we can win." She began to count out a cadence. "One and two and one and two and... Better?"

His reply was lost in the loud cheering of the spectators, but the pained look on his face wasn't hopeful. She glanced at the course ahead and shook her head. The finish line was close, but not close enough for a blue-ribbon win.

Charlie realized Mike's bad leg was giving out. It had to be his pride that kept him going on the one good foot he had left.

She sized up the situation. There was only one thing to do and, caring woman that she was, she was prepared to do it. Blue ribbon be damned.

She took a deep breath and deliberately made herself stumble. Thrown off stride, the inevitable happened. She tumbled to the ground and took Mike with her.

One more time, she found herself lying across Mike's chest. Eye to eye, nose to nose and lips to lips. In full view of all the other contestants and the laughing spectators who were cheering them on.

To her surprise, instead of reading her the riot act, Mike took her face between his hands. She was about to apologize for tripping him when he muttered something under his breath. Before she knew what hit her, he'd pulled her face down to his.

His mouth moved on hers, his searching lips outlined her own. His tongue urged her to open to him. Ignoring the time, the place and the incongruity of kissing a man she wasn't even sure she cared for, she sighed and gave herself in to the kiss she must have subconsciously wanted.

To her surprise, his kiss was not only unlike any other she'd ever experienced, it was everything she'd ever dreamt of. Only, never with Mike Wheeler.

As soon as this was over, she told herself, she intended to find out just how she really felt about him. And, more to the point, why she kept falling all over him every time they got together.

The rope that bound them together finally gave way. She gave in to the sensations sweeping over her and slowly and deliberately kissed him back. This was no ordinary kiss, she thought, as the world tilted and swirled around her before it finally settled back into place.

For a moment, she lay there gazing into Mike's eyes. He looked as surprised at finding her in his arms as she was to find herself there. Question after question began to run through her mind.

Did Mike know she'd deliberately caused the fall that took them out of the race?

Was he as surprised as she was by the kiss? At the way they seemed to fit together?

"Is everything all right? You're not hurt, are you?" she asked when she could finally speak.

"Damned if I know," he answered with a shaky laugh. He struggled to his feet and took her with him. "I guess I should apologize. I should have known better than to try to kiss you."

Charlie smothered a reply. *Try* to kiss her? How would his kiss have tasted if it had been a real kiss?

She tugged at the hem of her suddenly too-brief

shorts and brushed leaves from her hair. "No apology necessary. It was just a man-woman thing, right?"

"Right!" He agreed but he didn't look as if he believed it. She wasn't sure she believed it, either. Up until this moment, they hadn't been exactly friendly. Or even close to being real friends. Even knowing that, nothing had changed. All she could think of was how right it had felt when he'd kissed her.

She smiled at the laughing spectators. After today, no one would believe her if she told them she and Mike weren't in a relationship. It was a darned good thing she actually believed in miracles, she told herself as she made her way up the slight slope. If Mike realized she'd deliberately made sure they couldn't finish the race, it would take a miracle for him to believe she had an ounce of sense in her head. Or to trust her.

Mike felt like a fool as he shrugged and forced a grin for the benefit of their interested audience. All he could think of was the way Charlie had responded to his kiss—first with wonder and then with enthusiasm. She had enough passion in her for him to know something had changed between them, but he'd be damned if he understood what, or why.

A man-woman thing? Maybe.

He'd been around the block a time or two and recognized passion when he felt it. And, man that he was, he hadn't been all that surprised when he'd responded to the look in her eyes.

What she'd been thinking of when she'd deliberately tripped him made him wonder. Charlie might be inclined to think and behave in ways that drove him nuts, but today's events were over the top.

No doubt about it, he mused as he watched Charlie join the crowd. He was going to have to find out what had been behind the incidents that kept sending her into his arms.

Considering the way he and Charlie had felt about each other before today, maybe it was only a game. Or was it?

Chapter Five

Mike's conscience hit him where it hurt. He'd already decided to save Charlie from herself before Simons had given him the bad news about the two threats against Charlie for her part in the Blair House shooting. It was no longer a question of saving Charlie from herself—it could be a matter of her life and death. Considering the circumstances, romantic games weren't an option.

When he, as the Special-Agent-in-Charge of Security at Blair House, had been assigned the watch, he'd been all for telling Charlie, to warn her to be on alert, but the brass had been adamant; the threats were to be kept secret in order not to spook her.

The idea, he'd been told, was for her to go on with her normal activities. The problem as far as he was concerned, was that nothing about Charlie's method of operation was normal. Who else but Charlie would have a zoo in her backyard?

As for that kiss. Mike tried to put it in perspective.

It had been impulsive and definitely a mistake. How could he dismiss the kiss as merely a man-woman thing when it had been a soul-stirring romantic moment? How could he have forgotten his duty so far as to exchange a passionate kiss with a woman he was assigned to protect?

He might have felt apologetic when the kiss was over, but he wasn't really sorry—it had been too damn satisfying to dismiss it as a mistake. As to why it happened, clumsy, he was not—except when he was around Charlie. He knew damn well she'd been the one to make sure they would be disqualified from the race.

Sure as hell, this last "accident" had to have been one in a series of "accidents." If he counted the unusual finish of the relay race and the accident on the Baronovia palace grounds three months ago, this had been the third time he'd been her target.

No, sir. He wasn't ready to chalk the accidents up to fate, either. More than likely, Charlie had deliberately tripped. Why? In order to help him salvage whatever pride he had left after winding up on his aching buns only moments before? He should probably thank her, but the truth was he felt like a damn fool.

He bit back the realization that he owed her. No matter how tender his leg or how his rear ached, he couldn't just walk away even if he'd wanted to. Not until the State Department traced the perpetrators behind the letters and released him from the assignment. The only option left for him was to control his libido.

There was a problem. After today, he would never be able to look at Charlie without remembering the way she'd first hesitated and then thrown herself into his impulsive kiss—and left him wanting more.

Impulsive! Hell, he'd never had an impulsive moment in his life before he'd met Charlie Norris. The awful truth was that, at the rate they were going, she threatened to change his life.

The tour of the zoo was bound to take Charlie's attention off him, he thought gratefully when he heard an announcement over the bullhorn. There couldn't possibly be a way for her to cause any further damage to his psyche or his body during the zoo tour.

As for the tour itself, he wasn't too happy about that, either. Not when he had to keep an eye on her, on Jake and the surroundings, all at the same time. The idea of petting animals, babies or not, that Charlie had mentioned as inhabitants of the zoo made him uneasy. His experience with animals, domestic or otherwise, hadn't been happy.

"What kind of pets did you have when you were growing up?"

Charlie's question shook Mike out of his reverie. Anyone with a backyard zoo of her own was bound to think everyone had owned a pet or two sometime in their lives. He shook his head. "Nope. I was raised in a high-rise apartment in New York. My playground, the streets. No backyard, no pets."

Charlie stared at him in disbelief. "Never?"

"Never." He'd never even had a nodding acquaintance with any animals—except for the drug-sniffing dogs used by the Drug Enforcement Agency he occasionally came in contact with. For that matter, his brief, unhappy experience while on a special assignment with the U.S. embassy in the Philippines four years ago had cured him of being around anything that didn't walk on two feet, but he wasn't prepared to tell her so.

Still, this was a different time and a different place, and he had his son to consider. It was long past time for Jake to learn how to live in a world with animals and pets. The idea of Jake petting the animals in Charlie's private zoo made him uneasy, but he'd promised the kid, and a promise was a promise.

She gave him a long, silent look of sympathy before her helper Freddie called her and she walked away. Jeez, he thought with a grimace. The last thing he wanted was for Charlie to feel sorry for him. As far as he was concerned, he was doing just fine. Or had been, until she came along with her off-the-wall ideas.

He glanced around the grounds for Jake. Sure enough, the boy had attached himself to Charlie. He headed in their direction and promised himself that from now on he would stick to his job of protecting Charlie instead of having any romantic ideas about her.

"You still want to go on the tour, Jake?"

"Sure, Daddy." Jake's eyes lit up with enthusiasm. "Miss Charlie says she has a baby kangaroo in her zoo! She's going to let me hold him."

"I'm not so sure about that," Mike said dryly as he visualized a diapered kangaroo cutting loose to hop around the compound. "He's not exactly the cuddly type."

Jake's lower lip quivered. "Miss Charlie says he is."

"Miss Charlie says and does a lot of things," Mike agreed and eyed Jake's smiling companion. "You just have to learn to take what she says and does with a grain of salt."

He hoped Charlie got the message; if it were up to him, from now on kissing was out.

"Salt? I don't got any salt." Jake searched the pockets of his overalls. "Can we go get some?"

Mike smothered a laugh at the worried expression on Jake's face. He'd do well to remember Jake was in the literal stage of growing up and took everything he was told seriously. "No, no salt. I just meant you can't believe everything Miss Charlie says or does."

Jake looked puzzled.

Charlie's eyebrows shot skyward, a smile curved the corner of her lips. If he'd tried to intimidate her, it was obvious she wasn't buying.

Mike began to feel like a jerk. He'd intended to remind Charlie she was the last person to be a role model for his small son. All he'd managed to do was to put his foot in his mouth and risk antagonizing the woman he was supposed to protect. If he intended to stick close to her without giving his assignment away, he'd better stay on speaking terms.

"Zoo time!" The voice of Freddie, a high-school student, sounded over the bullhorn. "Everyone line up two by two and follow Charlie Norris. And please, don't touch the animals unless she tells you it's okay."

Mike took Jake's hand and fell in line.

Charlie felt Mike's eyes boring into her. She didn't have to look back at him to know what he was thinking, or what was behind his oblique remarks to his son.

He was thinking about their kiss.

So was she.

She shivered as she recalled the way his maleness had stirred her when she'd fallen on top of him. The surprised expression on his face as he'd gazed up at her. How that look in his clear blue eyes had deepened when he'd pulled her down to meet his searching lips. The way he'd delved into her mouth as if he couldn't get enough of her. How the air around them had seemed to still. And how, for an incredulous moment, she'd felt they were the only two people in the universe.

What had started out as a well-intentioned reason to keep Mike from losing the race and his pride along with it, had backfired and turned into something more. The deep personal and sensuous exchange of the kiss had made her realize she was not only attracted to Mike, she wanted him as a woman wants a man. For sure, after that embrace and that kiss, she would never be able to forget him.

Her body warmed at the lingering electric shocks of desire still coursing through her veins. And at the way her heartbeat had changed from a sedate waltz to a rapid two-step.

She'd momentarily forgotten he was the man she'd intended only to tease, to humanize. Forgotten they were in full sight of a cheering audience. And found, to her surprise, that she hadn't really minded the public display of affection.

Impossible, she told herself. She hadn't been particularly interested in Mike before now. A lawman hadn't been on her most-wanted list.

And yet, today she'd discovered the truth. Lawman or not, she hadn't been able to get enough of Mike or his kiss.

Even now, she felt so shaken inside, she couldn't look at him. Not without asking him to kiss her again and, this time, to turn it into something more than a kiss.

Wrong place, wrong time, she scolded herself. And maybe, in spite of his strong attraction, the wrong man.

"We're here at the zoo," she announced when they reached a wooden fence. "Remember, no petting unless I tell you it's okay. Some of the animals are new and unaccustomed to humans." She swung open the gate to a chorus of promises.

Charlie laughed when Boomer spotted her and bounded to meet her. Nothing could take a person's mind off problems faster than the trust and unconditional love of animals. Boomer was no exception.

She knelt, took the little kangaroo into her arms and rubbed its nose. "This is Boomer," she said to her interested audience. "He's actually a wallaby, one of the forty varieties of kangaroos. In Australia, male kangaroos are called boomers."

"Why 'boomers'?" One of the guests wondered out loud.

"I'm not sure, but it's probably because of the noise they make when they get excited," Charlie answered. "Of course, my little guy is still quite young—he's just a baby. We'll have to give him time to grow up before he gets his full voice."

Jake pulled at Mike's hand. "See? I told you Miss Charlie had a kangaroo, Daddy."

"Yeah, well don't forget he's just to look at."

Mike threw a cautious look at the wallaby and hoped it didn't remember him. ''We don't know how tame he is.''

Boomer, looking over his owner's shoulder, caught sight of Mike. To Mike's chagrin, he bounced out of Charlie's arms and hopped straight toward him.

Mike cussed under his breath. It was beginning to look as if the animal had taken on one of Charlie's habits and was going to knock him down. He took a step backward—too late. Before he could brace himself, Boomer bounded into the air and launched himself straight at him!

The burst of laughter and the encouraging shouts from the bystanders galvanized the other zoo animals into action. An avalanche of ducks, geese, chickens, a pig and a goat scattered by, around and through Mike's feet.

Mike staggered backward, bounced off a man aiming a camera at the action and wound up falling flat on his back with Boomer sitting on his chest and, Mike was ready to swear later, grinning at him. Like it or not, they were eye to eye, nose to nose.

Mike swallowed hard and tried to grin back. Hell, the mammal must have remembered him from the time he'd found it hanging in a tote bag on Charlie's office coatrack waiting for its feeding, and somehow associated him with its next meal.

Mike looked around for Charlie and fought to

catch his breath. Whatever the kangaroo thought Mike had to offer, it sure as hell wasn't dinner. It was also clear that it *had* inherited its owner's unfortunate habit of knocking him over.

The crowd around Mike whooped, Jake bounced up and down, laughing. Mike frowned. His sense of humor didn't improve when Charlie plucked Boomer off him and offered a hand to help him up.

"Thanks a bunch." Mike caught himself before he told Charlie just what he was thinking about being knocked over by her *and* her pets. It was important that he stayed on Charlie's good side if he was to keep an eye on her. He dusted himself off and frowned at what looked like the zoo's entire population milling around them.

"Where did you get all these animals, anyway?"

"Here and there," Charlie said as she patted Boomer on his shoulder. "They either wandered in by themselves or people got tired of them as pets and brought them here. Some were sick and were given to me to nurse."

"Nurse?" Of all the things Mike would have associated with Charlie, he hadn't considered her nursing animals back to health. But then, why not? Wasn't it her trusting and caring nature that kept getting her into trouble?

"Yes," she said just as a large, black bird flew on to her shoulder and chattered in her ear. She made cooing noises and smoothed its feathers with a gentle forefinger. "Petey had a broken wing. He can fly now, but it looks as if he's decided to stay here with his friends."

Mike glanced at the odd conglomeration of birds and animals wandering around the enclosed area. In addition to the loose animals, he spotted a pot-bellied pig, two elderly turtles, an iguana and a squat, furry four-legged animal he recognized as a chinchilla. Off to a corner and hidden by the tree, he was ready to swear he'd caught a glimpse of a deer.

"Looks as if you have a deer on the premises, too," Mike said as he held on to Jake's hand. Lions and tigers came to mind as he began to wonder just where Charlie's collection ended. "Don't tell me that's legal around here."

"Well, not exactly." She bent over to pat a squealing pig nuzzling at her ankles. "Actually, the deer just wandered on the property. I didn't have the heart to call the animal shelter. I had to let it stay."

"In other words," Mike said, interested in spite of himself, "anything that walks in or is carried in here gets to stay?"

"Of course," she answered, surprised. "I would never turn anything or anyone away that needed help."

Mike started to reason with her, to tell her that that attitude of hers was one of the reasons she kept getting herself into murky waters. To his horror, he caught sight of a large snake in a cage and felt himself blanch. "Not again," he muttered and started to back away.

"You're not afraid of snakes, are you?" Charlie looked so aghast at the idea, Mike didn't have the will to confess he was. A man had to be a man, especially when the chips were down. No matter what.

"Not exactly," he said with a shudder. "Let's just say I'd just rather not be around them. Not after…"

"After what?" When he didn't answer, she went on, "This snake can't possibly hurt you. In fact, its…"

"Forget it." Mike felt silly after a look of compassion came into Charlie's eyes.

"Why? Talking about what bothers you might make things better."

Mike hesitated. Maybe she was right. At any rate, Jake was looking up at him and waiting for his answer. He didn't want to come off as being afraid of animals and he didn't want Jake to be fearful either.

He squared his shoulders. It was a story he hadn't thought about in a long time, but something in the way Charlie gazed at him compelled him to unburden his soul. That was another thing about her that bothered him—she was able to get to him faster than anyone else ever had.

"It happened a long time ago," he began slowly.

Images of a past he would rather forget became clear again. Too clear. His heart began to pound.

"It was in the Philippines," he went on, after he made sure no one was lingering within earshot. While many of them knew him as a Secret Service man, some members of their families did not. The less people knew about him and his past, let alone his weakness, the better. "We were trying to locate one of our men. He'd been targeted by a renegade band and disappeared overnight." He shuddered at the memory of what had come next. Nor could he bring himself to go into detail about what they'd found in the jungle two days later. "Suffice to say, snakes were involved. I sure as hell haven't wanted to look at another one since then."

"Don't worry, you won't have to after today," she said. "Let's keep moving." She hefted Boomer to one shoulder and held out a hand to Jake. "Come on. I want to show you my horses."

Mike tried to ignore the pleading look in Boomer's eyes as he hung over Charlie's shoulder. No way and no how was he going to encourage the little guy's devotion. Charlie could have him.

"You have horses, too? Can I ride one?" Mike almost tripped over Jake when he suddenly came to a halt. Between introducing Jake to the world of Charlie's zoo and getting knocked off his feet repeatedly, it definitely wasn't his kind of a day.

"Some day, but not today," Charlie answered,

with a quick glance at the frown gathering on Mike's forehead. "I have three horses. I have one I know you're going to love as much as I do."

Mike managed a smile. The affection clear in Charlie's voice and the pride on her face as she spoke about her collection of animal pets told him more about Charlie Norris than he'd ever thought to learn.

She wasn't only running a petting zoo, she was running an animal orphanage and maybe even an animal hospital.

No matter how he looked at it, it was beginning to look as if keeping an eye out for Charlie and keeping her safe was going to be a bigger job than he'd thought.

He would have to watch out for a possible dangerous human element that might be out to get her, and he had to make sure no one would use her care and compassion for all living creatures to get close to her.

Gazing at the way Charlie was charming the animals and the picnic guests in the waning afternoon sunshine, he made a vow to himself. Guarding her from possible assassins came before anything or anyone else, including him. If someone actually went through with their threats and tried to hurt her, it would have to be over his dead body.

With the realization of how he was actually beginning to feel about Charlie, there came the truth:

it wasn't Charlie and her different ways that had disenchanted him with people. It was the nature of his job.

Charlie was saying goodbye to the last of her visitors when Mike strolled up with a sleepy Jake in his arms.

"Gotta go. My mother's due back about now and cooking up a storm. Jake needs to get home for his dinner and before he falls asleep."

"Your mother?" It was funny how she was learning about Mike in bits and pieces. The more she learned, the more he became real. And the more real he became, the more she found herself attracted to him.

"Yeah," he smiled down at Jake. "Mom's the woman in Jake's life. She just lends him to me once in awhile."

"Lucky you. Everyone needs to have a woman who loves them in their lives." Charlie brushed Jake's hair off his face. "Especially little boys," she added softly when he smiled back at her. It was so easy to give her heart away to the miniature Mike.

Mike's gaze locked on hers with an intensity that made her shiver. The message in his eyes was definitely different than his usual enigmatic or disapproving look. It was something more than a look of concern. A something that disappeared as quickly as it had appeared once before. Only this time he didn't try to kiss her.

"Going to lock up now?"

Charlie nodded. "Just as soon as Freddie and I feed the animals and bed them down for the night."

"One helper doesn't seem enough," he answered with a long look behind them at the zoo. "Maybe I'll come back after I take Jake home and help out."

"No need, but thanks. We have it down to a science." She leaned forward and kissed Jake on his cheek. "I'll see you tomorrow."

Charlie thoughtfully watched Mike wave and leave. Now that she'd had a closer and more intimate look at him, she was ready to believe there was more to the man than she'd known before today.

Today's Mike wouldn't have been angry with her for giving the duchess Mary Louise her JAG lover's address. He wouldn't have frowned on her suggesting they have a Frisbee-throwing contest in a public park. Nor would he have objected to their dancing barefoot under moonlit skies as he'd done several months ago.

Today's Mike seemed to be more reasonable, more friendly. But behind that facade, he had become more watchful of her in a nice way.

She sighed and turned back to the zoo. Tomorrow at work was soon enough to try to figure out who was the real Mike.

AS HE DROVE home, Mike couldn't get Charlie out of his mind. He should have realized long ago that

Charlie was in a class by herself, and that the odd way she had of doing things was her way of trying to do her job to please people, to make them happy.

Maybe it was his own job that had turned him into a man he didn't much care for. He'd been involved in law one way or another almost all of his adult life, and his experiences had largely been forgettable. He'd started out as a lawyer, had even flirted with joining the navy's JAG Corps before he'd decided the Secret Service was more his idea of adventure—a decision that had taken him around the globe and eventually cost him his wife.

Ellie had wanted the glamour of being married to a man in uniform, an openly admired hero whose fame would rub off on her. She'd been upset with him because he hadn't worn a more glamorous uniform than a dark suit, and hadn't shared his life as a Secret Service agent with her. According to Ellie, he was a stodgy, private man whose life lacked excitement, forcing hers to lack it along with his.

If he'd been able to tell her how dangerous and exciting his life as a Secret Service agent could be, she would have probably left him a lot sooner.

He pulled into the driveway of his home. The lights were on to welcome him, the tantalizing odor of his favorite meat loaf wafted out the kitchen door as he stopped the car. This was as close to a normal life he could give Jake, he thought as he looked through the rearview mirror at his son, now fast asleep belted in his car seat. But it wasn't enough. He was still in a dangerous profession and for Jake's sake things were going to have to change. But not just yet.

There was still Charlie to protect.

Chapter Six

"Ah, Mike, there you are. You're just in time. I've just taken a meat loaf out of the oven."

Pleased to see his mother in the kitchen cooking up a storm on a Sunday night, Mike paused to kiss her cheek. "I thought you had a bridge game tonight. You and Pete have another one of your 'differences of opinion'?"

Minna Wheeler dimpled. "Not at all. I just decided that tonight was a good time to make your favorite dinner. Besides, Pete's getting a little too sure of himself lately. I don't want him to take me for granted." Mike's mother's broad smile encompassed Jake, cuddled in Mike's arms. "The little one asleep?"

"Wore him out." Mike paused long enough to settle Jake more securely then moved on to Jake's bedroom. "Guess he's going to miss his dinner."

"Don't worry, I'll make him a peanut butter and jelly sandwich when he wakes up." Minna trailed

Mike into the bedroom. "You know Jake, he won't eat anything he doesn't recognize. He'd probably prefer the sandwich anyway."

Mike laughed. "You got it. Charlie filled him up on peanut butter in celery sticks for his lunch. The kid was happy as a clam."

"Charlie?"

"Yeah. Charlie Norris."

Mike's mother pulled back the covers on the bed for Mike to lower Jake onto the bed. She gently slipped off the boy's shoes and socks, tucked the blankets around his little shoulders and bent over to kiss his forehead. "Might as well let the little angel sleep. It would be a shame to wake him up."

Mike smiled at the picture his mother made as she leaned over her only grandchild. If asked, she would have been the first to deny her age, but he knew she was about to turn sixty, even though she looked an attractive forty-five. Her long-time suitor, Pete Langer, swore that Mike's mother, with her boundless energy, her variety of interests and her care of Jake during the week, had to be drinking from the Fountain of Youth.

With a last, lingering look at his son, Mike followed his mother out of the bedroom. The scent of onions and spices coming from the kitchen beckoned to him. He wandered over to the stove to study the pan his mother had taken out of the oven and sniffed appreciatively.

"Hey, Mom, you know this wasn't part of our deal, but this smells great. I appreciate all you've done to help with Jake, but I want you to have a life of your own. I thought we agreed the weekends belonged to you."

"Just as Jake belongs in my heart," she said with a sweet smile. "Don't worry about me," she added. "I manage to fit everything in quite nicely."

"Maybe, but you ought to be playing in your usual bridge game instead of being here cooking my dinner."

Minna Wheeler busied herself setting hot rolls and iced tea on the table. "Not to worry. Pete said he might drop in later. I just might invite him in for a two-handed game of bridge."

Mike gave in with a wry grin. He'd never won an argument with his mother and he didn't expect to now. If anyone could handle a dozen things going on at one time, it was his mother. He turned his attention back to the steaming meat loaf, surrounded by carrots and potatoes. It was enough to bring a grown man to his knees. "Real meat in there?"

His mother bristled. "Of course, real meat. Real vegetables, too. Why?"

"Nothing," Mike muttered. He poked at a corner of the hot meat loaf and licked his singed finger. "Some people actually think it's bad to eat meat."

"Vegetarians," she sniffed.

Mike grinned at the disdain on his mother's face.

She came from a long line of women dedicated to serving hearty food to her family and nothing would deter her. "Like Charlie."

Minna Wheeler paused in taking a bottle of ketchup from the refrigerator. "That's the second time you've mentioned that name. Who is Charlie? Does he work with you?"

Mike reached over her shoulder for a cold beer, took a deep, appreciative swallow and sat down at the kitchen table. After spending a mind-boggling afternoon at the Blair House picnic, the scented kitchen and the prospect of his favorite meal was welcome. "You might say so," he said dryly, "but the 'he' is actually a 'she.'"

Obviously more interested in the gender of Charlie than in serving dinner, Mike's mother dropped into a chair. "Oh? Tell me more about this 'she.'"

Mike took another deep swallow of beer and sighed. Dinner was going to be late, but he welcomed being able to talk about Charlie to the one person who wouldn't tease the hell out of him.

"Charlie is actually Charlene Norris, the concierge at Blair House," he began. He went on to tell his mother about the first time he'd met Charlie and her involvement in the love affair of Mary Louise, the Dowager Duchess of Lorrania and JAG Commander Wade Stevens six months ago.

He took care not to remind his mother that that was the occasion he'd taken a bullet in his leg.

He wasn't going to tell her anything more about Charlie, nor about the impulsive, heart-stopping kiss they'd exchanged. She would only start matchmaking. He knew better than to open a door he wasn't ready to walk through.

"My, the lady sure seems to be interesting." As if the thought reminded her Mike was waiting for his favorite dinner, his mother picked up Mike's plate, jumped to her feet and headed for the stove. Together with a heaping portion of roast potatoes and vegetables, she put two large slices of meat loaf on Mike's plate. "Vegetarian, did you say?"

"Yeah. Charlie gave me a veggie burger for lunch, but don't worry. I'm still a meat-and-potatoes man." He grimaced at the memory. "Sit down and have dinner with me, Mom. I'm starved."

His mother let him enjoy his dinner for a few moments, but from the long and thoughtful looks she gave him, he sensed she wasn't through with him.

"Go on, Mike. What is there so unforgettable about this Charlie that you can't seem to get her out of your mind?"

Everything, he thought silently. From the top of Charlie's silken hair to her manicured toes and everything in between. But he knew better than to mention his growing interest in Charlie and her unusual methods of operation. Or how, to his surprise, his feelings about her had begun to change—become deeper.

He *had* changed his mind about Charlie, hadn't he? Instead of thinking of her as an annoying pain in the neck, he realized he was actually becoming fascinated by Charlie. Fascinated, but very aware the lady was a very desirable woman.

Otherwise, why would he have taken Charlie in his arms after she'd fallen on top of him and proceeded to kiss her as if his life depended on it? Not a mere peck on her inviting lips, either. Without even stopping to think, he'd gone as far as the circumstances had allowed. Somehow the kiss hadn't been enough. He would have wanted more if they had been two people in another time and another place. And if they hadn't been surrounded by at least fifty pairs of curious eyes.

He chewed thoughtfully and listened to his mother chatter away. No way was he prepared to bare his soul. Not when she'd been after him to remarry. If not for his own sake, she kept reminding him, then for Jake's. As much as she insisted she enjoyed Jake, she'd firmly maintained the boy deserved a home with a full-time mother and father. Even a sibling or two.

"Mike?" His mother tapped her fingers on the table—a sure sign her patience had run out.

"Sorry. What was the question?"

"I asked you what there is that's so unforgettable about Charlie."

"Yeah. Well, for one thing, we both work at Blair House." He rubbed his forehead and tried to get his thoughts together without giving himself away.

He went on to tell his mother about the small zoo Charlie kept in her backyard, including the story about the little kangaroo she'd brought to work that seemed to have attached itself to him.

His mother laughed. "With stories like that, no wonder you can't forget this Charlie." She sobered, glanced at the hall door that led to Jake's bedroom. "But is she good for you and Jake?"

"Sometimes," Mike said, more disturbed by the question than he cared to be. He had to be honest with himself and his mother. "Not always."

Minna started to gather the soiled dishes. "If you want my opinion, I suggest you'd be wise to forget the lady."

"Easier said than done." Torn between the effect Charlie was having on him and the need to think of her as merely an assignment, Mike sighed. The events surrounding Charlie were moving so fast, his head was spinning. First the attempted assassination, then the threats against Charlie's life and now, his assignment as her bodyguard.

Sensing he hadn't been entirely fair to Charlie in the past, he carried his dish and cutlery to the sink.

Was Charlie good for him? For Jake?

The longer he thought of the puzzle that was Charlie, the more he realized she *was* good for him and for Jake, too. After all, they came as a package deal.

Apparently able to see the world through Jake's young eyes, she'd pretended to be his mother so that Jake could participate in the mother-and-son foot race. The proud look on Jake's face when they'd actually won the race was something Mike would never forget.

She made Jake laugh. Without a mother, Jake needed all the laughter in his life he could find.

Charlie's charm, wit and her eclectic collection of pets made him laugh, too. Considering that he'd seen more of the dark side of life than most people, her ability to help him see the amusing side of life was nothing short of a miracle.

There was also the way her hot body, her sweet scent and her sparkling blue eyes made him ache to kiss her senseless again. And this time to take her somewhere private where he could take her to bed. Foolish dreams, under the circumstances.

Overriding all his thoughts about Charlie's appeal were the two threatening letters Simons had shown him. His superior hadn't ordered him to make Charlie's care a full-time job, but Mike felt it was his duty to keep an eye on her well beyond today's picnic.

He glanced at his watch. There was still time

enough to check on Charlie before the night was out. He wanted to make sure her house was firmly locked and that all callers were known to her. "Think you can take care of things for a while, Mom?"

Her hands in soapy water, his mother looked over her shoulder. "Going out?"

"Yeah. Forgot something." He stopped. Thinking that two people were better than one lonely one, he said, "Take my advice, Mom. If Pete shows up, forgive him his sins."

MIKE BURNED UP the highway on his way to Mc-Lean and Charlie. She and her part-time assistant had to have finished putting the inhabitants of the zoo to bed. Freddie would be long gone by now. What bothered him was that Charlie was alone.

But not for long, if he had anything to do with it.

He pulled into her driveway, noted that the house lights were out and got out of the car. Stopping only long enough to make sure there were no signs of life around the perimeter of the house, he rang the doorbell. Once, twice. When there was no answer, he banged his fist on the door. He was just about to go around to the back of the house and try the back door when the door was flung open and Charlie stood there glaring at him.

She would have been naked if she hadn't had a towel wrapped around her.

It didn't help his hormone level to see her blond

hair twisted and precariously anchored on top of her head. The towel that covered her from her neck to the middle of her shapely thighs looked as if it were about to slide off. Drops of water clung to her suntanned shoulders. From the surprised look on her face, she obviously hadn't been expecting visitors any more than he'd expected to see so much of her. Words froze in his throat.

"Mike?"

He motioned her inside, followed her and closed the door behind him. "Why didn't you answer the door when I rang the doorbell?"

Suddenly aware of Mike's searching gaze, Charlie clutched the towel more closely around her. Heat spread south from her waist.

Why hadn't she answered the doorbell? It was a heck of a question coming from an uninvited guest. She caught her breath, her eyes narrowed. "In the first place, I wasn't expecting company. In the second place, I was in the shower. When I finally heard your knock, it sounded as if someone was about to break down the door." She paused for breath and glanced over his shoulder. "Where's Jake? Is something wrong?"

"He's fine; at home with my mother." He looked around the room. "You *are* alone, right?"

Charlie's radar finally connected with the set look on Mike's face. Darn! It was obvious that the old Mike was back—in spades. Where was the man who'd pulled her on top of him and taken her lips in a kiss that she undoubtedly would remember for the rest of her life?

With Mike's apparent return to his old persona, the golden glow left by the kiss began to fade. This man wasn't the one she'd started to fall in love with. In his place was the self-centered, judgmental tyrant whose personality was light-years removed from her own. "I'm not sure it's any of your business, Mr. Wheeler, but I was just about to go to bed." She paused for effect. "Alone."

"Not before I check the windows and doors to make sure they're properly locked." Mike started for the nearest window.

Charlie caught his arm. She knew by now that Mike was paranoid about security, but enough was enough. "It's one thing for you to throw your weight around Blair House, but that's not good enough around here. You can't just barge in here and behave as if my home is a problem of yours."

When Mike silently gazed down at her, she pushed away. "Wait right here. I'm going to put on some clothes. We'll talk about this when I get back."

Charlie disappeared into her bedroom, but knew enough about Mike to know he wasn't going to remain glued in place to the spot just because she'd told him to.

She listened for his footsteps on the polished

wooden floor and told herself she should have been angry at Mike's intrusion. She would only have been fooling herself. She wasn't about to admit the truth to Mike, but whenever she felt his presence, she felt safe. Tonight was no different. If there *were* a security threat involving her, Mike was the man she wanted to have with her.

Mike was disturbed by Charlie's angry reaction to him. He had come here intending to tell her her home was not only a security problem, but she was the prime target. Knowing how Charlie ignored security issues, he would have to make her understand, whether or not she wanted to believe it.

Sure, Charlie was too trusting, too friendly, too willing to make everyone happy. Those traits were part of her charm.

As he wandered around the room checking the window locks, he could no more think of Charlie as Charlene than he could go on believing she was the cause of all the trouble she seemed to get into. Not when he saw her innocent blue eyes and realized he couldn't bring himself to say or do anything to bring fear into them.

There was no way he wanted Charlie to have to look over her shoulder afraid of what might happen next. If there were a problem involving her, security was his job. He intended to find some unobtrusive way to take charge.

While he waited for Charlie to rejoin him, Mike

checked the living room, the dining room, a small kitchen and double-checked the lock on the back door. He avoided the two closed doors, obviously bedrooms. The last thing he wanted was for Charlie to think he had an ulterior motive in showing up tonight.

He'd been a red-blooded American male in the past, he thought with a glance at the bedroom door. With Charlie in the picture, he was beginning to believe he could be again.

Under the present circumstances, it was natural for him to discover he wanted more than sex from Charlie. He wanted her respect, and more to the point, he wanted to start out a new relationship with her by being her friend. What might come next was something in the future he couldn't afford to let himself think of just now.

His conscience was telling him Charlie was his charge and her safety was his responsibility. He might have believed that if, intentionally or not, she wasn't doing a damn good job of driving him out of his mind—the mind that was saying no to erotic thoughts while his body said yes.

"Okay." Charlie walked up behind him, hands on her hips, fire in her eyes. "Talk."

She'd looked like a dream walking in her cream-colored short shorts and Blair House T-shirt at the picnic, but to Mike she looked even more enticing now. She'd changed into a sweat suit that covered her from her neck to her slender ankles. She smelled of scented soap and fresh water. Her cheeks were flushed and her body language spoke volumes; she was annoyed as hell.

No matter what she wore, he would always envision Charlie in a skimpy towel that left her shoulders and slender neck bare, hardly covered her thighs and revealed the intriguing swell of her breasts—breasts his fingers ached to caress.

So much for mere friendship.

He felt like a bigger fool than ever as she waited for him to speak. It took him only seconds to make up his mind to give Charlie another reason for his visit. She'd been through more trauma in the past few days than any woman should have to endure. There was no use ruining today for her, too.

"I...er..." He started over. "I came back to thank you for going along with my son for the mother-and-son race. And to tell you how much Jake and I enjoyed the picnic and zoo this afternoon."

The fire in Charlie's eyes faded as she sized him up. Even from the little she knew about Mike, she felt certain that thanking her for a nice afternoon wasn't the reason he'd shown up tonight.

She'd been as aware of the sexual tension that had hung between them this afternoon as he'd seemed to be. Judging from the way her body was reacting to the speculative look in Mike's eyes, that sexual tension was still there.

No matter the real reason behind Mike's visit tonight, from the way he was looking at her she could tell he hadn't forgotten their kiss any more than she had. Heaven help her, she could tell that he knew she wanted him to kiss her again.

Impossible! He might be attractive, intelligent, courageous and handsome, but he had a son and, from the hard look usually found on his face, ties to a past he couldn't seem to put behind him. More importantly, he seemed to be content to be a lawman. Whenever he'd put his life on the line, if she wasn't careful, her heart would be there, too.

"You wanted to thank me?" She couldn't believe what she was hearing. "What does that have to do with checking locks on the windows and doors? What's wrong with using the telephone?"

Mike shrugged helplessly. How could he tell her he wanted to make sure with his own eyes she was okay? She'd think he was a nutcase for sure. An involuntary smile hovered at the corner of his lips at his thoughts. "Chalk it up to another impulse. I didn't think you'd mind if I dropped by."

Charlie melted. Mike was referring to the kiss. If the man knew how his smile changed his too-somber appearance for the better, he'd not only smile twelve hours a day, women would be falling all over themselves to get close to him. She hoped he couldn't possibly be aware of the number he was doing on her.

"You're welcome," she managed. "I enjoyed Jake, too." Talking about his son was safe. No way was she going to discuss the kiss, what had prompted it, what could have been the reason behind it and what to do about it now. Not when the atmosphere surrounding her and the donor of the kiss was so heavy with sexual tension. "Is there anything else I can do for you?"

Mike's eyebrows rose, his smile broadened. She wanted to sink through the floor.

"A loaded question if there ever was one," he said. "Did you mean it?"

Charlie marched to the door, held it open and summoned her most regal pose. "I told you this afternoon, the kiss was a perfectly normal man-woman reaction brought on by the excitement of the moment. No matter how much I may have enjoyed it at the time, I haven't changed my opinion. Whatever you may think about it, it's over."

"Ah...so you enjoyed it?"

The pleased look on his face and the way he threw her words back at her was too much for her to bear. "Yes, but as I said before, Mr. Wheeler, it was a case of me woman, you man. That's all there was to it."

Mike knew better. He'd already sensed Charlie was as surprised by her reaction to their kiss as he had been at initiating it. Now wasn't the time to pursue the issue, damn his luck. Not only because Charlie didn't look in the mood, but he'd been charged with keeping her safe. Becoming emotionally involved with her now would not only be unfortunate, it was downright risky. He had to cool it, but he took comfort from knowing that at least their cards were on the table.

"You're right," he said. "We'll talk at your office tomorrow. And by the way," he said as he exited, "thanks again. For everything."

Her head spinning at the yearning look in Mike's eyes, Charlie locked the door behind him. Between what might be behind that warm look he gave her and his resolute goodbye, she wasn't quite sure what he had thanked her for.

Chapter Seven

Alarmed by what he'd seen at yesterday's picnic, or rather by the lack of what he should have seen, Mike headed for Simons's office first thing Monday morning. Intended as a decoy or not, he was damn sure Charlie should have been told about the threatening letters or, at least, the danger she might be in.

As far as he was concerned, it was an unacceptable situation.

After being admitted to Simons's office, Mike plunged right in. "With all due respect, sir, after checking out the picnic yesterday, I'm more convinced than ever Charlie Norris needs to be briefed on what's going on."

Simons looked up from the sheaf of papers he'd been reading. "Why? Something go wrong?"

"Depends." Mike briefed Simons about the unisex T-shirts worn by all the attendees. He emphasized the lack of identifying name tags, and the ease with which a troublemaker could have joined the picnic. Coupled with the zoo activity as a possible diversion, anyone could have done the unthinkable. The more he explained about what he considered the lack of security, the more concerned about Charlie he became.

Simons fixed him with an unsympathetic look. "Sounds to me as if you were looking for trouble under every rock. Considering that everything went well, you're overreacting, aren't you?"

"No, sir. All things considered, I believe that the person who wrote those poisonous letters could have easily mingled with our people yesterday. No one, including myself, could have stopped someone bent on making trouble."

Simons steepled his hands, leaned back in his upholstered executive chair and considered Mike. "Sorry, topside has decided the less Charlie knows, the better our chances are of catching the perpetrator. She has to act and react normally to be convincing. The brass feel that, under the circumstances, it would be wiser to have Charlie continue her normal duties as if nothing unusual has happened. She's a smart, capable lady. With you keeping an eye on her, I'm sure she'll be fine."

Mike was not only appalled at the game plan and its implications for Charlie's safety, he'd just learned something about himself. Somewhere along the line, the duty to protect Charlie had become personal.

He gritted his teeth to keep from swearing. There was no way he would be able to watch over Charlie twenty-four hours a day. Leaving her alone at night, to his way of thinking, was now out of the question. "In other words, sir, you're throwing an innocent woman into a duck shoot and damn the consequences. What if she gets hurt? Or worse?"

"So call it a duck shoot. At least it's a plan until we come up with a better one." Simons fixed him with a cool look. "Any objections?"

"No, sir." Privately, Mike had a lot of objections, but it was obvious from his superior's attitude that Simons wasn't about to listen to reason. From the look on his face, Mike's job was on the line.

It was time to talk to Charlie.

After a brief goodbye, Mike backed out of Simons's office and stalked down the hall to Charlie's. The door was open. Another security mistake. He bit back a comment as he entered. "Got a minute?"

Charlie glanced up and set the guest list for tonight's VIP dinner aside. "Sure. Come on in." Last night, when he'd said goodbye, he'd looked as if he'd wanted to kiss her. Not today. Today, his body language was back to being all business, the look on his face dark.

She'd never known a man quite like Mike Wheeler. After yesterday's heated embrace, she'd expected more from Mike than conversation. Her eyes were drawn to the firm line of his mouth. No man's kiss had ever affected her like his. No man's gaze had ever sent her thoughts to wanting more than one kiss, either.

Mike glanced at the empty coatrack beside the door. "The kid home today?"

Charlie smiled. "If you're talking about Boomer, the answer is yes. You don't have to worry. Fred's taking care of the animals today."

She didn't blame Mike for looking so apprehensive. Not everyone was able to take a diapered baby kangaroo in stride. Especially one as frisky as Boomer; after one look, the animal had apparently bonded with Mike.

Mike glanced warily around the office. "You don't happen to have any other pets around here, do you?"

"Only those in pictures on the wall. The rest are safely at home. Including the snakes," she added wryly. "You can come in now."

Mike felt his face blanch at the mention of snakes. After a cautious look around, he entered Charlie's small office. The walls were lined with framed yellow covers of the *National Geographic* magazine featuring animals. A snapshot of Boomer was propped up against her computer.

Mike sauntered into the office and closed the door behind him. Charlie's attempt to reassure him that she was alone gave him the opening he'd been waiting for. Once he convinced her she needed someone at home with her at night, he wouldn't have to worry about her. She might not take kindly to the idea, but he intended to make damn sure the someone was a member of the Secret Service.

"I meant to talk to you about safety," he began. "It looked to me as if between this job and taking care of animals, you have your hands full. Don't you think it's about time to hire a permanent helper? Maybe someone who lives on the grounds?"

"I wish. Not on my salary." She studied him for a moment, unable to reconcile her memories of the man who had kissed her so passionately with the man who sat here today. "Is that what you wanted to talk to me about —my animals?"

"Not entirely." Mike gestured to the chair in front of the desk. "Okay if I sit down?"

Charlie waited until Mike made himself comfortable. She noted the crisp line of his shirt, the shine on his leather shoes, the regulation haircut and navy-blue suit. He was so strict with himself, so professional.

"So, tell me," she said. "Weren't my answers about the shooting incident clear enough? Or did you have something else on your mind?"

She'd already realized this wasn't a drop-in, spur-of-the-moment visit. As for what Mike had in mind, after seeing the set look on his face, she didn't think this was going to be a discussion about the kiss, either.

The warm feeling she'd begun to feel for the new Mike took a back seat. The man sitting in front of her and regarding her with a serious expression couldn't possibly be the same man who had kissed her. Nor could he be the warm and smiling father of the little boy she'd taken into her heart. This was the old, businesslike, serious Mike. A man who saw shadows lurking everywhere and who looked as if he saw one lurking in her office now.

She bit back a sigh. "Let me guess. I've done something else that displeases you?"

"Not you. Not exactly."

She waited, resolutely bent on returning his intent gaze. One of them had to get to the reason for this morning's visit out in the open, and it looked as if it was going to be her. "If there's a problem you wanted to discuss, as I told you yesterday, sometimes sharing a problem helps to make it go away."

"Yeah. Maybe." Mike settled back into his chair, but he couldn't seem to make himself comfortable. Charlie looked so honest, it was difficult to believe she would knowingly hide something about the shooting. He had to find out if subconsciously she'd seen something incriminating without realizing it, but he couldn't do it here. Not when he was deliberately disobeying an order by discussing the case with her. Simons, or for that matter anyone, might overhear.

How to get Charlie to talk about the shooting

without telling her why he wanted to know? How to tell her he'd been assigned to protect her? Unfortunately, he was no closer to being able to warn her now about the threats against her life than he'd been last night.

He mentally cursed the top brass's decision to keep Charlie out of the loop. He had to find a way to protect her without violating his sworn duty.

"How about dinner tonight?"

"Dinner? You waited until this morning to ask me out to dinner?"

Charlie looked at him as if he'd lost his mind. Considering that he must have come off like a testosterone-driven teenager asking a girl out on their first date, maybe he had.

"Yes, I am." He shifted uncomfortably in his chair and tried a hopeful smile. He saw a frown crease her forehead. The smile wasn't working.

"Why now?"

"Last night I was afraid we'd gotten off on the wrong foot." For a thirty-five-year-old widower with a son almost four years old, he must be sounding more like an idiot.

Maybe he *was* an idiot for thinking Charlie could be interested in going out to dinner with him. After grabbing her, kissing her as if his life depended on it and now behaving as if nothing had happened, maybe he was out of his mind. Bad idea.

Yesterday at the picnic, he'd been surprised by

the number of people Charlie considered her friends. After spending an afternoon in her company, he could understand why. She was warm-hearted and friendly. So why not with him?

Friends, he mused with a thoughtful look at Charlie. Maybe friendship was the logical approach.

''To tell you the truth, since we work at Blair House together, I figured it was time for us to become friends instead of adversaries.''

Friends! What was left of Charlie's good humor tanked. Just when she'd decided Mike was the first man in years to make her dormant hormones sit up and take notice, he had to come up with this idea— friendship!

Suspicious of his motives after his behavior at the picnic, she sat back and gazed at Mike. He was trying to look as if asking her out to dinner was a routine matter, but she wasn't buying. Not when he looked as if he wished he was anywhere but here talking to her. She'd be darned if she was ready to be friends with a man who kissed as though she was the only woman on earth for him and the next moment asked to be her friend.

''For one thing, I can't go—I'm on duty tonight,'' she replied. ''For another, I don't understand why you'd ask me to go out with you. You've been on my case ever since we met almost a year ago.''

Mike was almost speechless. Considering the way he'd behaved since they'd met, she was right.

"You're going to have come up with a better reason if you really expect me to go to dinner with you," Charlie went on. In her book, the kiss hadn't come under the heading of mere friendship. It had been more a suggestion of something big to come.

"Give me a break," Mike finally sighed. "At my age, asking a woman out on a date isn't easy."

Charlie leaned across the desk. "Don't ask me to feel sorry for you, Mike. Accepting a date with a man who's made no bones about his disapproval isn't easy, either."

Mike glanced over at the coatrack. For the first time since he'd walked into Charlie's office, he wished Boomer were here. At least the little guy could have been a good conversation ploy. This conversation wouldn't have been started in the first place if he'd had his wits together. "Would it help if I apologized?"

"Maybe," she answered and eyed him thoughtfully. "Give me a minute to think about it."

Mike was all too aware Charlie Norris was no fool. Granted, she'd said she'd think about accepting his apology for being an ass, but he couldn't wait for her answer. He had to learn more about what had been behind the shooting and learn it now.

He needed to tell Charlie about the threatening letters, or find another way to get her to talk about the incident. In the meantime, he wanted the laughing Charlie back.

When was the last time he'd seen Charlie laugh?

At the picnic.

When was the last time Charlie had looked at him as a woman looks at a man she's attracted to?

At the picnic.

When, against all reason, had they done the man-woman thing?

At the picnic.

He knew damn well Charlie had tripped them to save his pride. As to why he'd kissed her as though his life depended on her believing she was the one woman in the world for him, he didn't have more than a clue. As his mother would have said, he was probably falling in love.

His body warmed even now as he remembered Charlie hadn't even stopped to question him before she leaned into his kiss.

He might be slow to catch on, but he wasn't a dummy, either. Details about Charlie's reaction to the kiss began to add up. She would never have returned the kiss if her heart hadn't been in it.

The idea they might care for each other was as new as it was forbidden. A good agent was sworn to keep his emotional distance from his charge in order to do a good job.

On the other hand, considering Charlie's enthu-siastic reaction to the kiss, maybe it was a good place to start after all. He'd just have to remember the dinner date had to be the foundation for friendship and not for a romance. Even then he sensed it wasn't going to be easy being only a friend to Charlie. She was the woman he was beginning to want with every fiber of his being.

"I don't have any ulterior reasons for asking you out," he said quietly. "I just thought we could be friends."

Charlie sensed there had been a change in Mike, but she couldn't put her finger on it. Not when his magnetic gaze pierced her heart like a dart piercing its target.

It would serve Mike right if she turned him down. If only something in the tone of his voice and in the look in his eyes didn't tell her he was trying to be honest with her and with himself.

She bit her lower lip. It was as hard for a man to change as it was for a leopard to lose its spots, but maybe Mike meant what he said. Considering he'd admitted he'd been wrong about her and was trying to make up for it, maybe she owed him a second chance.

"Deal," she said. She rose and walked around to his side of the desk. She gestured to the small pile of papers waiting for her. "That is, if tomorrow night is okay with you. I have to work at a State Department award dinner tonight." She held out a hand for him to shake.

Mike took her hand in his and, in spite of his good intentions, gave in to temptation. His intention might have been to seal a friendship but he was surprised to discover a handshake wasn't going to cut it. There *was* that man-woman attraction between them.

Gazing into Charlie's luminous blue eyes, he was tempted to forget friendship and to take advantage of her open manner. He was tempted to draw her to him, to hold her so close he could feel the warmth of her lush body against his. To kiss her slender throat, her tempting lips.

Except he knew that in his mind, if not in his heart, he would be going too far with the woman he was sworn to protect. And, in the end, if they became too close, he might wind up violating her confidences in order to save her life.

He held Charlie's hand to his lips for a moment before he let it fall. "I'm afraid I was out of line for a minute there. Sorry."

To his regret, a shuttered look came over her eyes. "I'll go to dinner with you, Mike, since for some reason it seems so important to you. But the next time you decide to play games with me—no, don't bother to deny it, you have—you'd better mean it. You can pick me up here in the office tomorrow at eight."

"Right." Mike left the office thinking that Charlie's words sounded more of a threat than an acceptance to a dinner invitation. He should have known a kind and affectionate woman like Charlie would have picked up on the way he hadn't bothered to lecture her about the open office door when it was his second nature to have done so.

Except that he wasn't playing games—not by a long shot.

He would have taken the time to show her how he'd changed, only warning bells were already ringing.

TONIGHT WAS his chance to talk to Charlie. At his suggestion, his mother had decided to visit her sister in Florida, taking Jake with her.

He studied himself in the mirror. He felt strange, like a teenager on his first date. Hell, he'd been so undecided as to what to wear, he'd changed his clothes twice before he'd decided on a dark blue suit, white shirt and blue striped tie. Dressing up was probably better than dressing down.

Talk about dressing down. His thoughts turned to the vision of Charlie in that brief towel last Sunday night. He had to smile. At least tonight, she would be wearing more than a towel

ALL IN ALL, Mike thought things were going well when Charlie took a last sip of coffee, folded her napkin and looked him in the eyes. She was gorgeous in that slinky green silk dress and definitely all woman. If she had any secrets to keep, they weren't showing.

"Now that dinner is over, what did you want to ask me?"

He could have pretended he didn't know what she was talking about, but that wasn't the way he operated. In his book, he called a spade a spade. He was just waiting for an opening.

"How do you know there was something I wanted to ask you?"

"I'm a people person, remember? You've been waiting all evening for an opening." She waved away the waiter when he offered a dessert menu. "Go ahead, ask me."

Mike smiled his surrender. "I was hoping you'd tell me what happened the day of the shooting at Blair House."

"I've already told you."

"Tell me again."

"Why?"

"I'm hoping you'd forgotten some detail that would be helpful. For my final report, that is." Thank God he hadn't given away the truth that she was a decoy and that he'd been assigned as her bodyguard. That would have spooked her for sure.

Charlie glanced at the small red scar on her wrist, her memento of the shooting and shuddered. "How could I have forgotten something like that?"

Mike lifted his coffee cup and gestured to the hovering waiter for a refill. "You'd be surprised at what people forget in a moment of stress. I'm counting on your help. Pretend I'm hypnotizing you. Walk me through the events, please.''

"Like what?''

"Close your eyes and tell me what you see.''

Charlie closed her eyes, leaned back in her chair and tried to picture the moments before the shooting. "I see General Negri approach my desk. He has a leather briefcase in one hand and is carrying his overcoat over his arm. He stops to ask me if a Mr. Oberhammer is still in a meeting in the library. I answer yes and tell him the meeting is about to break up.''

"Go on,'' Mike said softly. "What happened then?''

"Mr. Oberhammer comes out of the library. The general seems to recognize him. He asks me to introduce him to Oberhammer. I do. Before I know it, the general starts to shoot.'' She opened her eyes. "That's all. Does that help?''

Deep in thought, Mike nodded. "You say the general was carrying an overcoat over his arm?''

"Yes.''

"He probably was using the overcoat to hide the gun. How many shots did he get off?''

Charlie closed her eyes and tried to visualize the scene again. "One.''

"And he managed to hit both Mr. Oberhammer *and* the plaster angel over the mantle with one bullet?''

Charlie's eyes opened wide. Excitement ran through her as Mike's question registered. "The shots must have come from two different people!"

"Right," Mike agreed. "Who else is in the picture?"

"Maybe it was his aide-de-camp," Charlie added slowly.

"Aide-de-camp?" Mike picked up on something they all could have missed. "I don't remember seeing a man dressed in a foreign military uniform near the shooting when I showed up. Are you sure?"

"I'm sure. He was with General Negri, but disappeared during the struggle for the gun."

"What did he look like?"

Charlie stopped to think. "He was a dark man of medium height and wore a uniform with a lot of yellow braid over one shoulder."

Mike prodded Charlie's visual memory. "The same uniform as the general's?"

"I think so, but I'm not sure. I was too shocked by what was going on."

"Try to remember."

Charlie hesitated, then her eyes lit up. "Both uniforms were the same as the uniform the Prince of Baronovia wore when he was here."

Mike took a long swallow of his coffee wishing it had been something stronger. "Baronovia," he repeated slowly. "Probably another disgruntled Bar-

The Harlequin Reader Service® — Here's how it works:

Accepting your 2 free books and gift places you under no obligation to buy anything. You may keep the books and gift and return the shipping statement marked "cancel." If you do not cancel, about a month later we'll send you 4 additional novels and bill you just $3.99 each in the U.S., or $4.74 each in Canada, plus 25¢ shipping & handling per book and applicable taxes if any.* That's the complete price and — compared to cover prices of $4.75 each in the U.S. and $5.75 each in Canada — it's quite a bargain! You may cancel at any time, but if you choose to continue, every month we'll send you 4 more books, which you may either purchase at the discount price or return to us and cancel your subscription.

*Terms and prices subject to change without notice. Sales tax applicable in N.Y. Canadian residents will be charged applicable provincial taxes and GST.

If offer card is missing write to Harlequin Reader Service, 3010 Walden Ave., P.O. Box 1867, Buffalo NY 14240-1867

NO POSTAGE
NECESSARY
IF MAILED
IN THE
UNITED STATES

BUSINESS REPLY MAIL
FIRST-CLASS MAIL   PERMIT NO. 717-003   BUFFALO, NY

POSTAGE WILL BE PAID BY ADDRESSEE

HARLEQUIN READER SERVICE
3010 WALDEN AVE
PO BOX 1867
BUFFALO NY 14240-9952

GET FREE BOOKS and a FREE GIFT WHEN YOU PLAY THE...

Lucky 7
SLOT MACHINE GAME!

Just scratch off the silver box with a coin. Then check below to see the gifts you get!

YES! I have scratched off the silver box. Please send me the 2 free Harlequin American Romance® books and gift for which I qualify. I understand I am under no obligation to purchase any books, as explained on the back of this card.

354 HDL DRNC

154 HDL DRNS
(H-AR-11/02)

FIRST NAME   LAST NAME

ADDRESS

APT.#   CITY

STATE/PROV.   ZIP/POSTAL CODE

7 7 7	**Worth TWO FREE BOOKS plus a BONUS Mystery Gift!**
🍒🍒🍒	**Worth TWO FREE BOOKS!**
♣♣♣	**Worth ONE FREE BOOK!**
🔔🔔🍒	**TRY AGAIN!**

Visit us online at www.eHarlequin.com

Offer limited to one per household and not valid to current Harlequin American Romance® subscribers. All orders subject to approval.

© 2000 HARLEQUIN ENTERPRISES LTD. ® and TM are trademarks owned by Harlequin Enterprises Ltd.

DETACH AND MAIL CARD TODAY!

onovian national. Someone who doesn't want anyone to know he's still in the United States.''

Charlie shuddered.

''Who had the most to gain by shooting a United Nations representative? Who had the most to lose if he were caught?'' Mike wondered out loud. He glanced over at Charlie. Her eyes were wide with shock. ''I hate to have you worry, but I want you to be aware of the fact that what you've remembered could be dangerous.'' He covered her hand with his own and squeezed it to reassure her.

He didn't say so, but he intended to take care of the problem before Charlie realized she *was* the problem.

What he didn't say was that the missing shooter had to be the same person who had written the threatening letters.

Chapter Eight

Determined to find the author of the threatening letters before Charlie discovered she was someone's target, Mike headed for Simons's office again.

Simons was polite, but that was the best thing Mike could say about their meeting. Hiding his frustration, he wound up his case by recounting what Charlie had told him last night. "So you see, sir, it appears there was a second shooter—someone who wants to remain unknown. I believe he's behind those threatening letters and I'd like you to authorize my doing whatever it takes to find him."

Simons motioned to Mike's report of the shooting lying on the corner of his desk. "You don't say anything about a second shooter in there. Are you sure?"

"Yes." Mike tried his best to be patient, but his temper was rising fast. As far as he was concerned, Simons was a typical bureaucrat so tangled up in red tape he couldn't move, mentally or physically.

"That's because Charlie didn't remember seeing him at the time I first interrogated her. She only recalled him while we were having dinner last night."

Simons's knowing smile and quirked eyebrow burned Mike. He had a feeling what was coming next and he damn well didn't like it.

"Dinner? Together with Charlie? Do you think it's wise to become involved with someone you've been assigned to protect?"

Mike bit back a sharp retort. Of all the bits of information he'd fed Simons, the only thing that appeared to concern the man was the dinner he and Charlie had shared last night.

"Frankly," Simons went on, "I'm afraid your concern for Charlie has muddied your thinking, Mike. Until we have some kind of proof there was more than one man involved in the shooting my advice to you is to keep things cool. We don't need any complications. Understood?"

For a moment Mike was tempted to tell Simons just what he thought of him and where he could put his advice. Except that he was honest enough to admit Simons's comment had a measure of truth in it. One of the Secret Service commandments was that its operatives remain objective and detached from the people they were duty-bound to protect.

What he did take exception to was the assumption

he'd ever let his growing interest in Charlie get in the way of his sworn duty.

"Understood, sir."

The fact that he was tasked to take care of her even as he was falling in love with her might have complicated matters, but as far as Mike was concerned, it didn't change a thing.

Mike exited Simons's office before he made their encounter up-front and personal. He didn't need Simons to give him permission to try to save Charlie's life, damn it. What he did need was a good idea where to go for help, and it wasn't going to be with Blair House's security unit. Not with Simons digging in his heels.

Mike spent the next twenty minutes analyzing the problem. If, as he suspected, a disgruntled Baronovian national was involved, the place to go for help was the newly established U.S. embassy in Baronovia. USN JAG Commander Wade Stevens was in charge of helping the marine unit put security procedures in place, courtesy of his father-in-law. Stevens was bound to understand his request for information.

The commander owed him one, Mike mused as he strode back to his office. He'd not only helped Stevens rescue his duchess and her father from an earlier assassination plot, he'd taken a bullet in his own leg in the process. It was pure luck that the bullet hadn't done greater damage than leave Mike with a leg that ached under stress. It was aching like hell now.

To keep things under cover, Mike decided to contact JAG Commander Dan O'Hara, Stevens's best man at the royal wedding. If anyone knew how to contact Stevens without drawing attention, it had to be O'Hara.

"YOU WANT ME to do what?"

For a moment, Mike thought O'Hara was going to jump out of his skin. Afraid they were attracting the attention he'd hoped to avoid, Mike glanced around the busy coffee shop where they had arranged to meet. "I want you to get in touch with Wade Stevens for me," he repeated. "But I'd feel a hell of a lot better if you kept your voice down."

O'Hara bit into a warm Danish and followed it up with a swallow of hot coffee. "You don't want much, do you?" he said. "I'm a navy JAG lawyer, same as Wade. My job is to investigate, defend or to prosecute the law of the sea. Where exactly does that request of yours come in?"

"I'm asking you because you're Stevens's best friend, and because Stevens is currently stationed at our embassy in Baronovia. I can't afford to have anyone connect me with this inquiry."

"Why? I thought that is what you guys are supposed to do."

"Not if the inquiry is in danger of becoming personal. And, before you ask, I'm afraid it's headed that way.''

O'Hara peered at him over his coffee cup. ''I must be as crazy as you are because all of this is beginning to make sense. Run that idea of yours by me again.''

''I want, no I have to have Stevens get me the names of any Baronovian military nationals who might still be dissatisfied with the recent diplomatic agreement between our countries. And that includes our new embassy.''

O'Hara grimaced. ''It doesn't sound any better the second time around. Do you mind telling me why?''

''Only if you promise not to repeat it to anyone except Commander Stevens.''

''Sounds heavy. You sure?''

''It is, and I am.'' Mike eyed the tall, sandy-haired JAG lawyer. His navy-blue uniform with gold braid was attracting attention from female shoppers. If O'Hara was as sharp as his friend, Stevens, the request for covert information was in the bag. ''So, what about it? Are you going to help me or not?''

O'Hara drained his coffee cup and eyed Mike. For a minute, Mike was sure O'Hara was about to turn him down.

''It depends. You have to tell me more.''

Mike told him about the latest shooting at Blair House and the missing third man. He went on to relate Charlie's innocent involvement in the shooting. "I figure if I can find the missing shooter, I can clear up the threats to Charlie."

"Charlie? Charlie Norris? The one who…"

Mike cut him off. He wasn't in the mood to recycle Charlie's past escapades. Now that he finally understood her, her earlier escapades were peanuts compared to what she was involved in today. "One and the same."

"Ask me why I'm not surprised. If anyone could wind up in a situation like that, it would have had to be Charlie." He stopped laughing at the look Mike gave him. "I'm just surprised you'd go to such lengths to help her. The lady had you tied in knots the last time I saw you together at Stevens's wedding."

"Yeah." Chagrined, Mike frowned at the reminder. "Things begin to look different when you get to know the real Charlie. If you take the time to understand what motivates her, in some weird way she begins to make sense."

He went on to tell O'Hara about the Blair House picnic, Charlie's zoo and how much fun he and Jake had had that afternoon. He even brought up the aborted three-legged race. He knew better than to tell O'Hara about the kiss.

"Sounds as if you've finally eased up and developed a sense of humor, Mike," O'Hara remarked. He stood and brushed some crumbs off his pristine navy-blue uniform. "Okay, I'll do it. But if it's that hush-hush, I'll have to use special channels to get in touch with Wade. I'll get back to you as soon as I hear something."

Mike shook O'Hara's hand. "Thanks. I owe you."

"Don't forget that when I come calling," O'Hara said dryly as he waved goodbye. "You never know."

Mike left the coffee shop realizing O'Hara had been right about the change in him. Not only had he developed a sense of humor, he'd fallen for a woman who would undoubtedly drive him crazy before they were through. It was just a matter of time.

MIKE NEEDED TIME, and time was something he didn't have. Without Simons's cooperation, he'd have to take over the job of keeping an eye on Charlie by himself. Knowing Charlie's independent nature, it wasn't going to be an easy job. Hell, he thought as he headed for her office, he'd tackled more difficult assignments than this and come out in one piece. All he had to do was to be friendly.

"I'll be following you home tonight," Mike blurted as he walked into her office.

In the process of locking her desk, Charlie stared at Mike. "You're what?"

"I'll be following you home tonight," he repeated.

"Why tonight, may I ask?"

"Let's just say I plan on keeping you company."

"Sure you are," she said facetiously. "I've been going home by myself for years. Now, tell me the real reason."

"No particular reason," Mike replied. "Ready?"

"No." Charlie studied the tall figure that stood in her office doorway, hands in his suit pockets, an enigmatic look on his face. He was wearing the regulation black suit, white shirt and black tie worn by all Secret Service personnel while on duty.

More to the point, he'd never taken a personal interest in her before the recent shooting and, from the look on his face, he wasn't taking a personal interest in her now.

Charlie felt herself color as she recalled Mike *had* taken a definite interest in her at last Sunday's picnic. What troubled her now was, after that torrid kiss, there wasn't a hint in his current demeanor that he was aware of the sensual attraction that had sent her into his arms.

He was back to being the cool, poised Secret Service man he'd been before the picnic. So why did he want to follow her home?

"Where's your son?"

"With his grandmother. She went to visit her sister in Florida and she took Jake with her," he answered shortly. "If there isn't anything else you want to know, let's get going."

"As a matter of fact, there *is* something I want to know." She walked around her desk, came to a stop in front of him and waited until she had his full attention.

"It's seven o'clock, Mr. Wheeler," she began, "and I'm fully aware that you are no longer on duty. Neither am I. So, unless you have a personal reason that makes sense, I repeat, why do you want to follow me home tonight?"

He stared down at her without blinking an eyelash, but not before she caught a quick flash of emotion in his eyes. If he had a personal reason for wanting to see her home, it was obvious he wasn't going to share it with her. "Do you want to know what I think?"

He shrugged.

"I think you're back to being the old Mike Wheeler I used to know. The man who is always on duty, no matter what is going on around him. Well then, Mr. Wheeler, let me tell you something. I haven't done anything lately to warrant your professional attention. So, why me?"

Mike hesitated before he answered. He had to tell Charlie just enough to warrant his going home with her, but not enough to give away the existence of the threatening letters.

"I want to make sure there's no one hanging around your house. And that all your doors and windows are locked before you go to sleep."

''Does this sudden interest mean you think I'm really in danger?'' A hollow feeling filled Charlie's chest. First, because she didn't believe she had a personal security problem; she'd been watchful ever since Mike had warned her of a possible danger. And second, because she'd actually allowed herself to believe Mike was interested in her and cared for her. Now, it looked as if his interest in her was merely professional.

''If that's all you're interested in, I can take care of making sure everything is secure by myself.''

He shook his head, a shadow crossed his face. ''No. I want to make sure everything is secure personally.''

Charlie picked up on the *personally.* ''Not before you tell me why this sudden interest in my safety?''

''It's my job.''

Charlie's heart cracked. *Personally* hadn't meant anything personal after all. ''No, it's not, Mr. Wheeler Maybe during business hours, but not when I'm off-duty.'' She gathered her briefcase and purse and, without looking back, strode out of the office.

CHARLIE WAS HEADING OUT of D.C. on I-495 when she noticed the headlights of a car keeping pace with hers, slowing when she slowed, accelerating when she picked up speed. She chided herself for being paranoid and tried to dismiss the car. Until she turned off on SR-193 and the car's headlights turned also.

If only she'd swallowed her pride and let Mike follow her home!

She quickly reached for her cell phone and called 911.

She breathed a sigh of relief when she finally turned into her own driveway and saw the black-and-white waiting for her outside her door. Chiding herself for allowing herself to be frightened, she stepped out of the car, pushed the lock button on her car keys and turned to explain her fears to the police.

A car pulled into her driveway, Mike swung out of his black Lexus and grabbed her in his arms. "Shh, it's me, Mike."

"I...I thought you were one of those bad guys you're always talking about," Charlie gasped when she realized the car that had been following her had been Mike's. "How could you have frightened me like this?"

"I didn't mean to, but that should tell you something. I could have been anyone out to get you," Mike said as he held her close to him, so close he felt the rapid beat of her heart, the tiny hiccups as she tried to keep her fear from showing. He wanted to smooth her hair away from her forehead and kiss the tears away from the corner of her eyes. He couldn't, because matters *would* have become personal—just as Simons had warned him. Most of all, if things became personal, he would be useless to Charlie.

He dropped his hands, stepped away and turned to explain himself to the waiting police. After a few moments, they shook hands, got into their black-and-white and drove off.

Mike grimaced, shoved his hands into his jacket pockets and turned back to Charlie. "How about going inside? I'll check the doors and windows and get out of your hair."

Charlie tried to pull herself together, but it wasn't easy. She wasn't ready to forgive Mike for frightening her, but after this episode, she needed his presence and the warmth and safety of the house.

Mike trailed behind her. "The animals fed?"

"Yes, Freddie does that for me," she said as she tried to use the house key. Her hand was shaking so badly, all she could do was fumble at the lock.

Without a word, Mike reached over her shoulder, took the key out of her cold, almost numb hand, put it in the lock and opened the door.

By now, Charlie was so nervous, she could hardly think clearly. "It's been so hectic at work lately, I asked Fred to line up a few friends to take care of the animals for the next few weeks."

"That's a relief. Boomer, too?"

This from a man she'd decided had no heart? "Yes, of course. Why?"

For a moment, she could have sworn that Mike looked embarrassed over his voiced concern for Boomer. "Figured maybe the little guy is too young and too attached to you to be happy out there alone."

Charlie put her briefcase and purse on the kitchen table, turned on the lights and breathed a sigh of relief. The ride home, with Mike trailing her, had taken more out of her than she'd realized. "Boomer's not alone. He has lots of company, even a girlfriend, Lila. Don't tell me you care for the little guy?"

He flushed and, for a moment, seemed to become human. "Maybe, from a safe distance."

Grateful to have something to talk about that would ease the tension between them, Charlie smiled. "Maybe there's some hope for you after all. I was beginning to think you didn't care about anything except your job."

Mike froze in the act of checking a window. "No comment." He moved on to another window and glanced outside. "No yard lights?"

"Yes, of course. I had lights installed because of the zoo." She pointed to the light panel on the wall.

"No automatic timer?"

"I never thought I needed a timer," she said. "I'm usually home before dark."

Mike went over to the light panel, checked the identifying descriptions and pressed the proper button. A red light came on. "What's the red light for?"

Charlie came to his side and stared at the light panel. "It's been a while since I had the system installed. I think a red light means there's something wrong with the system."

Mike went to the window, pulled back the curtains and gazed outside. If it weren't for the full moon, it would have been pitch dark. "There's something wrong," he muttered as he closed the curtains.

Charlie shivered. "There's an emergency backup number someplace, but I'm not sure where I put it. I'll take care of it tomorrow."

"I'll call for you."

"No, thank you. *I'll* take care of it in the morning." She headed for the coffeepot, filled it with water and took a bag of ground coffee out of the refrigerator. "No way am I going to let you take over my life."

Mike silently went on checking windows.

"You're going to have to give me a good reason for all of this recent interest of yours," she said to the back of his head. "You're behaving as if I need a bodyguard."

He disappeared into the hall. Seconds later, she heard the front door lock rattle.

Charlie stared after Mike. He hadn't answered her, but from the expression on his face before he left the kitchen, she sensed she'd managed to hit the nail on the head. Mike *was* acting like a bodyguard!

She wasn't going to rest until he told her why. She waited until Mike came back into the kitchen. "Coffee's ready."

His eyebrows rose. "Inviting me to stay?"

Charlie recalled her mother's favorite saying: you can get more bees with honey than you can with vinegar. As much as she was angry with Mike, if ever there was a time to spread honey, this was it. "Yes, of course."

Mike silently pulled out a chair and sat down.

Charlie took two cups off the shelf of the maple hutch that occupied one wall, set them on the table and reached for the coffeepot.

Mike rose and took the coffeepot out of her hands. "Sit. You're liable to get burned."

"Isn't there anything you're not ready to take care of?" Charlie glared at the coffeepot as if it were guilty of some crime.

Not where she was concerned. Mike saluted her with his cup. "No big deal. It's only a cup of coffee."

"Only a cup of coffee," she repeated. "*And* following me home. And checking doors and windows and offering to take care of yard lights. You're not going to leave until you come clean with me. The danger you discussed at dinner was pretty vague. Exactly what is this all about?"

Mike was beginning to wish he were anywhere but here. He'd never had a nosier or more stubborn person to guard. If they'd been curious about his methods, at least they'd been too grateful to question why. Charlie, with her usual independent way, had to be different.

"You *are* my bodyguard, aren't you?" Charlie's eyes were wide with shock as she interpreted his silence. "Why me?"

Mike glanced at the doors leading to three bedrooms, one of them obviously Charlie's. He hadn't said as much when they'd discovered the yard-light control wasn't functioning, but he was damn sure there was something sinister behind the malfunction. Under the circumstances, it was too much to hope it was a coincidence.

"If you don't mind," he said, knowing full well Charlie's reaction was going to be off the wall at his suggestion, "I'll stay here tonight in one of your extra bedrooms. Maybe tomorrow, too, or as long as it takes to get the lighting situation straightened out. Just to make sure."

"Make sure of what?" Charlie replied. "My answer to your staying here tonight is 'Not on your life.' The answer to why you want to stay is a question—To make sure of what?"

Mike shook his head. When he'd become a Secret Service agent he'd made an oath not to reveal secrets or agency procedures, and he wasn't going to reveal them now. If he wasn't going to get his department's cooperation, he'd take care of protecting Charlie in his own way, Simons be damned, but he couldn't reveal those plans, either. "You're just going to have to trust me."

"Trust you when you're acting as if my life is at stake? And when you won't even tell me why?"

Silently, Mike studied Charlie. He'd been ordered not to tell her the whole story, but saving her life was precisely what he was trying to do. Nor could he tell her he suspected there might be another shooting any day, any time now, unless Wade Stevens and Dan O'Hara came through with the names of a possible shooter in time to cut the knees out from under the bastard.

"I'd like to stay," he said. "You won't even know I'm here."

"Fat chance," Charlie answered with a dark look. "You're not exactly the type to fade into the surroundings. But, if you insist..."

"I do."

Even as she protested, Charlie felt an inner calm. After the frightening drive home from Blair House, calling 911 and hearing the edge in Mike's voice, it was comforting to know he would be as close as the next room.

She would have been more pleased if the look on Mike's face wasn't so grim. Something about the way he looked at her told her she wasn't home free, not by a country mile.

"I didn't expect company for dinner," she said as she accepted the inevitable. "I was going to make a vegetable omelet for myself. There's fresh fruit compote for dessert. Would you like to share?"

Mike fought the temptation to decline Charlie's offer. Vegetables, in any shape or form, weren't his style, but there was no use antagonizing her any more than he had already managed to do just by being here. "Sure," he answered. "Just make my half plain—skip the vegetables."

"That figures," Charlie murmured. "If you'd like to wash up before dinner, the third door down the hall is the spare bedroom. I'll call you in twenty minutes."

"Can I help?"

Charlie looked at him over the refrigerator door and waved him away. "No, thanks, I'll be fine."

Relieved, Mike headed down the hall. Since his cooking expertise was basically limited to cold cereal in the morning, sandwiches at noon and heating up whatever his mother had left in his freezer at night, he hoped Charlie could cook.

So far, so good, he thought as he checked out the bathroom situated between Charlie's bedroom and the bedroom she'd indicated was his.

He couldn't have suspected that although he was

afraid there might be another shooting if O'Hara didn't come through in time, he, not Charlie, would become the target.

One more time.

Chapter Nine

"Coffee?"

"Sure." Mike pushed away his empty plate. The omelet, minus the cooked carrots and broccoli Charlie had put on her half, had been adequate, but for a man used to meat and potatoes, hardly filling. The fruit compote, heavy with strawberries and served with shortbread cookies, had been a step up. He was still hungry, but the truth was his was a different kind of hunger.

Charlie poured him a cup of coffee. "Sugar, cream?" A drop of fruit syrup lingered at the side of her lips.

"No, thanks," he said absentmindedly, his eye on the drop and the possibilities it presented. "Make mine black."

She handed him the steaming cup. "The better to stay awake?"

Mike shook his head as their fingers touched.

"Nope. I go for the real thing." He stared into her eyes. "Always."

He reached across the table, gently wiped the fruit stain away from the corner of her mouth with a forefinger and held it to her lips.

Charlie's eyes locked on his own. "So do I." She said softly. She licked the corner of her mouth and, in the process, his finger. "When do you think you'll make up your mind about me?"

The sensation of Charlie's soft tongue brushing his fingers as she licked her lips sent a burst of electric shocks through him. Make up his mind? About Charlie? He was pretty sure he had, but darn his luck, any idea of romancing her was out. His oath to protect her came first.

Mike gazed at the faint blush that had come over Charlie's face and decided a judicious retreat was in order. At least, while he could still stay out of trouble. He emptied his coffee cup in one last swallow. "I think I'll take another look around outside and turn in—that is, unless you'd like me to help clean up in here?"

Charlie's eyes clouded at the abrupt change in Mike. Just when she'd begun to hope tonight might be the night when they could pick up where they'd left off at the picnic, he was back to being withdrawn, distant. "No, thanks," she said. "Why don't you go do your security thing while I clean up? I'll see you in the morning."

"Security thing," Mike mused wryly as he left the house. It was a damn good thing she wasn't aware of the whole truth.

When he'd finished checking the outside perimeter of the house, Mike came back inside and disappeared into his bedroom. Still tense with worry, he undressed to his boxer shorts and undershirt, washed up and climbed into bed just in time to hear Charlie close her bedroom door.

Knowing Charlie was on the other side of the door and out of his reach was doing a number on him. Frustrated, he punched the pillows, but couldn't find a place for himself. Instead, he imagined her soft sigh as she settled into bed. Imagined he heard the rustle of the crisp, cotton sheets as she turned over and settled down to sleep. And, heaven help him, pictured how she would look if she were here beside him while he explored that man-woman thing Charlie had talked about at the picnic.

His reaction to the memory of the way Charlie's soft body had felt when she'd fallen on top of him was tame compared to the reaction he had just thinking about her.

He really heated up when he found himself wondering what Charlie wore to bed. Something brief that scarcely covered her golden thighs? Lacy on top, so sheer her suntanned breasts and velvet shoulders would be showing through? The same soft, enticing breasts that had crushed against his chest when she'd wound up sprawled on top of him?

If, he mused, by some miracle, Charlie was in bed beside him, this time he wouldn't stop with just a kiss. He'd plunder her soft, fruit-tinged lips and savor the taste of her. Run his hands through her sweet-smelling silken hair. Move on to kiss every inch of her throat, her breasts and her waist, her thighs.

He'd caress her slender body until they were both mindless with the longing that only the other could satisfy.

For a brief and guilty moment, Mike relived their erotic kiss. Considering how it fueled his imagination, dwelling on kisses, real or imagined, was turning into a big mistake.

Thinking about the imagined mistake crowded his boxer shorts. Restless, he knew he'd be in deep trouble if he didn't cool his thoughts and try to think of something less suggestive than a warm and willing Charlie in bed beside him with her soft scented hair spread across his pillow.

He was finally about to drift off to sleep when a series of loud bumps crashed against the wall of the house. He bounded out of bed, shoved his bare feet into his shoes, grabbed his holster and his gun and made for the kitchen. Seconds later, he heard Charlie's bedroom door open and she ran down the hall after him.

She was dressed in a short T-shirt, her long and slender legs bare, her hair flowing over her shoulders. To his surprise, she shoved by him and ran to the back door. Before he could stop her, she struggled to open the door and did a lousy job of it.

For a moment, it was almost as if his sensuous musings of how Charlie would look in bed had come true. He swallowed hard. "What's up?"

"It's Boomer," she cried. "I hear him outside trying to come in!"

Mike cursed under his breath. If everything was okay outside, Boomer and the rest of his friends would have been confined to the zoo area. Something was wrong, he could feel it in his bones. He checked to make sure his gun was in the holster he'd instinctively grabbed before he ran out of the bedroom.

"Here, let me help you." Mike had the back door open in seconds and Charlie ran outside. Mike glanced down at his boxer shorts and T-shirt, shrugged and followed her. Dressed or not, he wasn't about to go back in and get dressed and leave Charlie outside alone.

To Mike's amazement, Boomer came bouncing out of the shadows and bounded into Charlie's arms. "How in the hell did he manage to jump over the zoo gate?"

Charlie made soothing noises and patted Boomer on his furry back. "He couldn't have," she answered in between soft murmurs of assurance to the obviously shaken Boomer. "I don't understand what could have happened. The zoo gate is much too high for him. Besides, I keep it securely padlocked."

Mike's sixth sense kicked into overdrive. "Someone had to let him out!"

"It wasn't me, I was in bed." She looked at him over Boomer's shoulder. "Good Lord, if Boomer is out, what about the rest of the animals? They're probably wandering all over the yard by now. We'll have to find them before they hurt themselves or run away!"

Mike could see she was frightened, but not for herself. It was her animals she was worried about. A typical Charlie reaction. She cared more about others than she did herself.

"In the dark?"

"All we have to do is listen. We'll be able to tell where they are."

Mike peered into the darkness where the only objects he could see were trees and shadows. He listened intently. The eerie silence was unbroken, except for the sound of crickets and an occasional cluck from a chicken, a quack from a duck or a sharp bark from some unidentified animal. He shuddered. He wasn't about to ask which one.

As for the possibility of any other animals wandering around, if they were making identifying sounds, they were lost on him. Raised in a city, the only poultry he'd seen had been on ice in a butcher shop. As for kangaroos, horses, deer and the other assorted animals he'd noticed in the zoo, as far as he was concerned they belonged on a movie screen, not in someone's backyard.

He began to shiver, and it wasn't for the lack of proper clothing. Something sinister was out there in the darkness, or had been, or his name wasn't Mike Wheeler. Instinct told him this was part of the same scenario to frighten Charlie. It was working.

There was a problem: it was too damn dark and the area too large to do anything about looking for any clues tonight.

The sensible thing to do would be to put the search off until morning when he was fully dressed and after his wake-up cup of coffee. Unfortunately, he knew Charlie well enough by now to know she had a mind of her own. If he didn't help her find strays tonight, she'd be out here by herself. Possibly watched by the person who had let the animals out.

"Come on, Charlie," he said. "Use your common sense. It's too dark to see anything out here. You're running on emotion, not logic."

"Someone has to do something, and now before it's too late," Charlie insisted. "Are you going to help or not?"

Mike shuddered. "You actually want me to help find a dozen animals who might be loose? On a pitch-dark night? Without flashlights?"

"If that's your only problem," she answered with another pat on Boomer's rear, "I have a couple of flashlights stored in the broom closet just inside the kitchen door for emergencies."

Mike gave up. In Charlie's book, and maybe even in his if he were to be honest with himself, this *was* an emergency. Besides, it was a case of do it Charlie's way or no way. "Okay. Wait right here. And keep Boomer with you." Mike backed away. From the way Boomer was eyeing him, the little guy would be in his arms if he stayed.

Mike ran back to the house to get a flashlight. Every nerve in his body told him Charlie needed him more than she knew. It wasn't only the threatening letters that worried him. The inoperable outdoor lighting system and the unexplained open gate to the zoo had to have been manipulated by the same person who intended them as warnings, or worse.

He had to stay here with Charlie at least until he found who was behind these threats, even if it meant he was jeopardizing his career.

If it came to that, he told himself, he was willing to give up his career to protect Charlie.

He grabbed two flashlights and made his way back to where Charlie waited for him. His stomach tied up in knots at the possibility that there were things without feet sliding around out there, he asked, "How about snakes?"

Charlie eyed him with a grin. "Don't worry.

Snakes sleep at night. They should be in their cages.''

Mike didn't like the amused way Charlie was looking at him. It didn't help his ego, either, when Boomer looked at him with what seemed to be pity in his eyes. Damn! Even the little guy seemed to know Mike was on shaky ground. And, from the look in his expressive brown eyes, he actually felt sorry for him!

''Where do we go from here?'' Mike tried to avoid connecting with Boomer's gaze. The way Charlie held the kangaroo under one arm while she tried to handle the flashlight finally got to him. He sighed. ''Here, let me carry Boomer for now. He's getting too big for you.''

Charlie smiled gratefully and handed him the young kangaroo.

Mike was ready to swear that the little marsupial burrowed closer and began to purr like a cat. His little paws dug into the back of Mike's shirt as he held on for dear life. Mike sighed again. Boomer wasn't what he'd pictured in his arms tonight.

''Let's go over to the zoo gate. I want to make sure it's locked and there aren't any more escapees.''

As she spoke, Charlie studied Mike. He was bravely making his way behind her, shivering with each cautious step. With his chiseled features, broad shoulders, muscular chest and even in his underwear, he was handsome. And, considering he was on unfamiliar territory, possibly one of the bravest.

Which man was the real Mike Wheeler? she wondered as she shone the flashlight on the path and carefully made her way to the zoo. The stoic, self-assured Secret Service agent? Or the man who cared enough about her to brave the darkness, barely clothed, in order to protect her? And, with a clinging Boomer in his arms!

Charlie was so preoccupied with her warm thoughts, she tripped over a fugitive chicken. She screamed. The chicken squawked. Terrified, the chicken flapped its wings and waddled off into the darkness. To Charlie's horror, she tripped on her furry slippers. Crying her dismay, she threw out her arms to keep from falling.

Mike must have seen the accident coming. "Sorry fella," he said. He dropped Boomer, took a giant step forward and held out his arms to catch Charlie. "This is getting to be a habit," he said shakily. "Not that I mind," he went on with his lips buried in her soft hair, "but one of these days I'm going to decide it isn't an accident. And it's not going to stop with this."

Before Charlie could collect her thoughts, Mike lifted her chin and held her head with his hand. She looked up into his velvety blue eyes while he brushed her lips with his. He tasted of coffee and strawberry syrup and promise. All of her senses stirred as she threw caution to the winds and clasped her arms behind his neck. "And then what?"

He ran his other hand over her hip, lingered at her bottom and deepened his kiss until her head started to swim. "Later," he whispered softly into her lips.

Charlie took a deep breath. Whatever was going on was impossible. She knew better than to read more into the moment than Mike could have intended. She stepped away from him and pulled her T-shirt back down over her hips. "This isn't what we came out here for," she said, shaken by the way her skin was still tingling. "We have to find the animals before they get away."

His wry grin almost undid her. She reached for Boomer's paw. "Let's go."

Two hours later, after rounding up a few chickens and a duck or two, Mike made a makeshift lock for the gate. Charlie and Mike trudged back into the house. To her relief, the rest of the zoo inhabitants had obviously been too smart and comfortable to run away from home.

"How about a hot drink?" she asked Mike when they were back in the kitchen. "You look as if you could use one."

"Yes, thanks." He gazed around the room. "Something strong would be nice."

Charlie considered the contents of her pantry.

"How about some hot tea and brandy? I keep some for cooking."

His grateful look almost undid her.

"Why don't you get some clothes on while I boil water," she said. "Your goose bumps have goose bumps."

Mike turned away and headed for his bedroom. Goose bumps weren't all he had after seeing Charlie in the bright light of the kitchen. She didn't need a lacy nightgown to be inviting—the short T-shirt made her look as sexy as hell.

With his clothes back on, Mike made his way back to the kitchen. He'd already sensed it was going to be a long night, but he hadn't counted on the physical torture brought on by watching Charlie sitting at the table sipping hot tea and smiling at him over the rim of the cup.

Hell, he thought and forced his thoughts to a safer plane. After a heart-stopping couple of tense hours, Charlie merely looked friendly. He'd wanted to start out by being friends, hadn't he? Anything else would have to wait on the back burner.

He held the cup of tea between his hands and enjoyed the warmth. "Now, this is the way I see it," he began. She set her cup on the table and gave him her full attention.

"When I get back to the office, I'll call the company who put in your yard-light system and get it fixed ASAP. I'll also pick up a new lock for the zoo gate. I..."

"Hold it right there," Charlie said, her smile gone. "*I'll* handle the lights *and* the lock. I told you before, I can take care of myself."

"Yeah, sure." Mike emptied his cup and from the feisty look on Charlie's face gave up the idea of a refill loaded with brandy.

"I figure on following you home for the next few days and spending the nights here," he went on. "Just in case some more odd things happen."

"You wish," she snorted. "I know men and women live together all the time, but not me. I'm not too jazzed up about the idea of what people would think if you moved in with me."

"We won't tell 'em." Especially not Simons. Without waiting to find out who would have the last word, Mike stood and headed for his bedroom.

Charlie followed him, protesting all the way. "I don't need a human watchdog," she insisted.

"Maybe," Mike answered. "Think about your options. I'll ask you again in the morning. Goodnight."

MIKE CHECKED the luminous dial of his watch. Dawn? No such luck, it was just past four. He cursed as he squirmed against the mattress trying to find a comfortable place for himself. There wasn't any, nor, he suspected would there be as long as he kept picturing a warm and willing Charlie lying in bed beside him.

The last thing he remembered when he finally drifted off to sleep was the look in Charlie's eyes when he'd said goodnight for the second time. After spending the past few hours looking for wandering animals and making sure the gate was securely locked, she still looked delightfully fresh and seductive. It was all he could do to keep himself from making "later" now.

But the truth was he didn't have the heart to make love to her until he could make love the way she deserved.

THE NEXT TWO DAYS passed in a blur with Mike hearing zip from O'Hara. His days were spent at Blair House taking care of his duties and keeping an eye on Charlie as he'd been ordered to. His evenings and nights were spent helping out at Charlie's zoo because it was the only way he could make sure she was safe. Besides, he *wanted* to be near her.

He actually grew to know the animals by the names Charlie had given them and, to his surprise, found Charlie had been right. Animals could be satisfying friends. Snakes not included.

His nights were also spent sleeping yards away from Charlie and being driven out of his mind.

Until Friday, when the other shoe dropped.

"Glad you're alone."

Mike looked up to see Simons walking into his office. When the man closed the door behind him, Mike had a strong suspicion from the expression on Simons's face he wasn't happy with him.

Simons took a seat and, without any preliminaries, laid the reason for his visit on the table. "I understand you've moved in with Charlie Norris."

Mike drew a deep breath. "Not exactly."

So much for keeping his whereabouts the past two nights a secret. He didn't know how Simons had found out, but he was damn sure that after her reaction to his making himself at home, it hadn't been Charlie.

"How not exactly?"

"It's not what you think," Mike amended hastily. "It's my way of trying to make sure no one does anything else to intimidate or hurt Charlie. Or carries out the threats they made in the letters."

Simons cocked an eyebrow. "That's a new one."

"Believe it," Mike rejoined. "Do us both a favor and listen to this."

Mike went on to recount what had already happened the other day: the malfunctioning lighting system and the breaking of the lock on the zoo gate.

"Coincidences," Simons said dryly when Mike was finished. "But I have the reputation of the service to think about. As of today, you're off the case."

Mike protested. "In the first place, what I do in

my private life is my business. In the second, you're hanging Charlie out to dry!''

Simons scowled. ''What kind of a heartless fool do you think I am? I'll take care of the replacement. You occupy yourself here at Blair House. Lord knows there's plenty going on around here.''

Mike seethed inside over the change in his responsibility. Officially, he was still assigned to Blair House where he could keep a covert eye on Charlie. Unofficially, he knew Charlie needed more than ordinary surveillance. As for what he thought of Simons, he wasn't prepared to tell the man he was a fool, not yet. He'd just have to ensure Charlie's safety on his own—and without Simons's knowledge.

The last thing Mike wanted Simons to know was that he'd asked Dan O'Hara to speak to his fellow JAG lawyer, Wade Stevens. If he learned that someone at the proposed Baronovian embassy in D.C. was the second shooter, he'd take it from there.

''With due respect, sir, if you don't want me to protect Charlie, who will?''

Simons rose to leave and smiled broadly. ''That's where equal opportunity comes in, Wheeler. I've assigned Liz Harrington to the case. That is, if Charlie wants her to move in…'' He left the sentence for Mike to interpret, shrugged and left the office.

In his frustration, Mike slammed his fist on the desk. Without explicit orders to Liz, or if the decision to have a full-time bodyguard were left up to Charlie, Liz Harrington would be spending the nights sleeping at her own home and in her own bed. And that would leave Charlie unprotected. With Charlie so trusting, who knew what might come next? The idea left him cold.

Without being aware of it, he'd developed a protective feeling about Charlie—and, clearly, something more. Something so new and so precious, he was coming alive again.

Now was no time to try to analyze the unexpected and welcome feeling, but there was one thing about the situation that he did know. Somehow, and no matter what Charlie had to say about someone staying with her, he had to make sure Charlie wasn't alone. Not now. Not by day, or by night.

He'd have a quiet talk with Liz Harrington, explain the situation and get her promise to keep an eye on Charlie, whether Charlie wanted her around or not.

Simons and his orders be damned!

Chapter Ten

"Ready?"

Shaken out of deep thought, Mike looked up and frowned at his visitor. It didn't help his dark frame of mind to find Charlie standing in his office doorway. Worse yet, he had no ready answer to her question. None that would make sense anyway. How could he back off after he'd finally persuaded her to allow him to spend his nights in her spare bedroom?

At a loss for words, he stared silently at Charlie.

A teasing smile crossed her face. "How easily you forget," she said as she glanced at her watch. "It's six. I thought you'd like to know I'm leaving for home. So, are you ready to leave, too?"

Mike clenched his jaw and mulled over his chances of answering her question without putting an end to their new and promising relationship. After being adamant that Charlie wasn't to leave Blair House without him, how in the hell was he supposed to tell her he was no longer her bodyguard? That from here on out, she was on her own? Or that Simons had ordered him to stay away from her? An order that ended any more overnights?

He found it hard to meet her eyes and tried to act nonchalantly. "Yeah, well…I'm a little tied up right now. Why don't you go on ahead?"

"Alone?" Her sweet smile faded and she stared at him as if he'd suddenly become a stranger. "Changed your mind about my being in danger, have you?"

It seemed to Mike the light in Charlie's eyes dimmed as she spoke. He shook his head.

"Has it all been a game?" she asked quietly after a long moment of uneasy silence.

"No. I've been reassigned." Mike's heart plummeted south when Charlie's eyes turned cold at his curt reply. Sensing he'd just taken a giant step back in their relationship, he still had to push on. "You might say there's been a change of plans. Has Liz Harrington spoken to you about tonight?"

"Liz? What does she have to do with your spending tonight with me?"

Mike had to force himself to keep from taking Charlie in his arms and telling her the whole story. Including that she was the target of threatening letters and she was being used as a decoy. And, heaven help him, giving her the real reason behind his dismissal as her bodyguard. It would only embarrass her.

What would Charlie's reaction be if he did tell her the truth, he wondered. Would she be frightened? Or, worse, considering her propensity for getting into trouble, would she try to take matters into her own hands?

"You might say Liz has taken over the night shift," he said with a forced, reassuring grin. "She'll be staying with you for a few nights until…"

"The next few nights?" She studied him as if he'd taken leave of his senses. "Until what?"

"I have a few ideas," Mike said. He hoped to convince her she wouldn't be alone in this mess, to make sure she didn't try anything on her own. "Don't worry. I've got it covered."

Even as he spoke, he saw a fire ignite in Charlie's eyes. Rather than being teed off by her reaction to his honest attempt to reassure her, he found himself actually proud of her. Instead of being cowed by events that would have unsettled the average person, male or female, she looked ready to fight. To give her credit, he had a growing feeling whoever messed with Charlie would be in for the fight of their lives.

"I have something to say about who spends nights with me," Charlie said angrily. "Or *if* they stay. I'm no one's prisoner! And that includes you!" Her gaze was sharp enough to pin him to the wall.

"Come on, Charlie," he said jokingly, "you didn't seem to mind my staying with you for the past two nights.'' When her back stiffened, Mike realized his stupid attempt to lighten the situation had backfired, instead of appearing to ease Charlie.

A deeper emotion appeared in her eyes. ''Not when that someone was you,'' she said softly. So softly, Mike wasn't sure he'd heard her say it. ''I only let you stay with me because you had me convinced I was in some kind of danger,'' she went on, her voice choking. ''And because I actually thought you cared for me.''

''You were, and I do.'' Drawn by the hurt he saw shimmering in her translucent blue eyes, Mike caught hold of her hands. When she tried to draw away, he tightened his grip. It was now or never. ''I swear I've told you the truth.''

''Maybe, but not the whole truth. What are you hiding from me?'' she asked.

It was all he could do to keep from trying to kiss away the unshed tears that glimmered at the corners of Charlie's eyes. ''You'll have to trust me, Charlie. I wouldn't lie about something as important as this.''

''I don't believe you,'' She pulled her hands out of his and backed away. ''You've never allowed anyone into your life, except maybe your late wife or Jake. Why would I expect you to let me in now?'' She didn't wait for his answer. ''I should have had my head examined for allowing you to come within ten feet of me when we're not at Blair House.''

Even as she spoke the harsh words that made Mike's face blanch, Charlie hadn't meant to voice them. She did care for Mike. Fool that she was, she'd even started to believe that instead of regarding her as just another security challenge, Mike had actually begun to care for her.

"Don't bother worrying about me," she said. "I'll be fine without someone spending the nights with me. I've taken care of myself for years without a problem and I can still do it now."

She'd known Mike at work for almost two years, more in passing than up close until now, she thought unhappily as she left for home. She'd dismissed him as a man who sensed trouble everywhere, seen or unseen. As far as she could tell from his behavior, he lived and breathed security from the time he woke up in the morning until he went to sleep at night.

At the picnic last Sunday, she'd discovered he was a normal man, and she was a normal woman. And she'd realized that a strong mutual attraction existed between them.

She'd actually discovered there were two Mikes. The staid, businesslike man, and the warm, caring man she knew now. The last man she should have fallen in love with.

His chest aching, Mike followed Charlie to the door and watched his hopes for the future disappear. He ached to go after her. To make her believe him and in him. The only thing holding him back was that there was nothing he could tell her with certainty. And not without violating his oath.

He'd been in love just twice in his life, he mused as he turned back to his desk. Once with Ellie, his late wife. A woman who had told him he'd failed to be the husband she'd wanted. And now, the second time, with Charlie.

The idea that she was lost to him because he hadn't been allowed to be open with her made his blood boil and his heart break. Now that he'd found her, it looked as if she were lost to him, too.

He glanced down at the list he'd been making before Charlie had appeared. It was a list of possible suspects who might be after Charlie and why; not that he'd have any concrete leads until O'Hara came through.

He grabbed the sheet, balled it up in his fists and threw it into the wastepaper container. To hell with lists! He was through waiting. He had an appointment to keep at a coffee shop with JAG Commander Dan O'Hara. Dan would brief Mike on his progress. There was no time to waste. Every hour Charlie was by herself put her front and center into danger. He knew her well enough to know that even if she didn't look for trouble, it seemed to find her.

The telephone was out—too risky. Not only for O'Hara, but for him. Even the walls in Blair House could have ears.

MIKE DIDN'T RECOGNIZE Dan O'Hara in civilian clothing in the coffeehouse—not until O'Hara called to him. Mike acknowledged him and made his way through the crowded room.

Dan was a genial, outgoing and trustworthy man; too honest to be anyone other than the man he appeared to be; a lawyer in the U.S. Navy's Judge Advocate General Corps.

In jeans, open-necked white shirt and brown casual jacket instead of his regulation blue naval uniform, the man still had a compelling presence. O'Hara was the type of man who would always stand out in a crowd.

When the three of them had worked on the Baronovia caper together, Mike had been sure Charlie had had a thing for Dan. If not for Dan himself, then, like most women, for the man's glamorous uniform.

Mike glanced down at what he was wearing. Hell, his standard, and no doubt boring, black suit, white shirt and black tie was a uniform, even if it was worn by Secret Service personnel. It had a look that enabled agents to fade into their surroundings. Maybe not the kind of uniform that had women falling all over themselves, but still a uniform.

Finding Dan and Charlie were only friends had been a relief. Discovering he'd been jealous of O'Hara should at least qualify him as human. Military uniform or not, he was still a man with all the needs and desires that came with the territory. Traits Charlie had as much as said he didn't possess.

His unusual relationship with Charlie kept taking one step forward and three steps back. She was as vibrant as he was staid. Together, at least in his opinion, they made the two halves of a personality destined to become one. Unfortunately, at the rate he was going, it was beginning to look as if he would never make Charlie believe they belonged together.

He signaled Dan to wait until he ordered two cups of coffee and brought them to the table. Hands full, he carried O'Hara's favorite Danish in a small paper bag between his teeth. He dropped the paper bag on the table in front of O'Hara and handed him a cup of hot black coffee. "Going incognito?"

O'Hara shrugged. "I'm on my own time. Besides," he said glancing around the café, "the last thing I need is for anyone to recognize me when I'm with you."

"Thanks," Mike muttered. "You sure know how to hurt a guy."

Dan shrugged. He opened the paper bag, investigated the pastry and nodded his approval. "I have to tell you that if the JAG knew what I was up to, he'd serve my head up on a platter. Face it, my friend, this whole business smells of foreign intrigue—not exactly JAG business."

Mike slumped into his seat, slipped the top off his

paper cup and stared into the steaming coffee. "My wanting to take care of Charlie isn't exactly Treasury Department business anymore, either."

"It's not?" Dan choked on his coffee. "Then what's this secrecy all about?"

"I've been taken off the case for reasons I won't go into," Mike said. "But as long as Charlie is involved, I'll go to hell and back to keep her from becoming an innocent victim. Topside and their rules be damned. They ought to realize Charlie was only trying to do her job and had nothing to do with the shooting."

O'Hara chewed his Danish thoughtfully then cleared his throat. "If I remember correctly, last year you didn't like the way the lady was doing her job."

"There must be a lesson in here somewhere," Mike muttered into his coffee. "Something about not rushing to judgment."

"You like Charlie!" O'Hara grinned.

Without thinking, Mike took a swallow of hot coffee, cursed and spit it out. "Damn, that's hot!"

O'Hara murmured his sympathy. "Men in love should never be left on their own. Thank goodness I'm not involved with anyone."

"That's only because some woman hasn't convinced you she's meant for you." He paused and gingerly touched his lips with his tongue. "I've got to find some ice."

"Yeah, sure. Take your time." O'Hara sat back to wait while Mike stalked off to drink out of the water fountain.

The background chatter and the sound of piped-in music grew louder. By the time Mike came back to the table carrying a cup of ice cubes, O'Hara had to lean closer in order to make himself heard. "Back to business. I assume you called me here to learn what I dug up?"

"I was trying to be polite," Mike said as he crunched on an ice cube. "What's the latest?"

Dan emptied his coffee cup and shoved it aside. "Unfortunately, not what you think. But Wade and May have moved up the date they'll start for home. Wade signaled he'll try to have an answer for you when he gets here next week."

Mike groaned. "Why not now?"

"Too sensitive. Besides, May, I mean the duchess, wants to be in on events."

Mike's spirits improved a notch. He remembered the lovely royal with a fondness he hadn't dared to voice while he'd been assigned to guard her last year. Praise would only have encouraged her to try some of the wilder enjoyments D.C. had to offer.

The Dowager Duchess Mary Louise of Lorrania and his Charlie were cut of the same cloth, he thought, not too fondly at the moment. They were both brave, strong and determined to play a part in their own destiny. On that note, he shuddered at

May's request to be present when finally he busted the suspected writer of the threatening letters.

"Sounds as if the duchess and the commander have found out something important."

O'Hara swallowed the last of the Danish and carefully wiped a few crumbs off the front of his shirt. "Sounds about right. But, if I were you, I'd cool it until they get here."

"Cool it!" Mike grimaced. "How can I cool it when Charlie's life may be in danger? My gut is burning up enough inside me as it is."

"Try," O'Hara answered. "No use spinning your wheels when you might not have to."

Mike shook his head. "The longer I wait, the closer Charlie comes to the inevitable day when the missing shooter decides the only way to keep her quiet is to get rid of her."

IT DIDN'T HELP matters when his boss caught up with Mike via phone.

"Since you're at loose ends," Simons's voice announced, "I want you to report to the State Department safe house right away. There's a VIP who needs to have your special attention for the next few days. We don't want anything to happen to him."

Mike glanced at the calendar behind his desk. "On a weekend? I had a few things planned for today." *Like watching over Charlie.*

"So, unplan. There are no weekends in this business, Wheeler, you know that as well as I do. Working around the clock comes with the territory,'' Simons added dryly. "Got it?"

"Got it,'' Mike replied reluctantly before he disconnected. Simons had to be commended for doing the right thing by people he thought were in danger. Too bad he didn't feel the same way about Charlie.

It was no time to drag his feet. The sooner he reported for duty, the sooner he might be able to come home. He sent an e-mail to Charlie, locked up his desk and headed for the safe house.

"'HAVE TO BE GONE for a few days. Call you when I get back.''' Charlie read aloud as she stared at the computer screen. The e-mail was unsigned, but she knew the message had to be from Mike—a first from a man who'd often warned her there was no privacy on the Internet. Why he'd chosen it to contact her this way was a surprise.

Why not in person?

Why did the message make her feel as if he intended to distance himself from her?

Ready to face the weekend, she curled up on the couch with a cup of hot chocolate in her hand and a plate with tangy orange slices and a peanut butter and jelly sandwich beside her. Her eyes were on TV's CNN, but her mind was on Mike and the dinner she'd intended to make for him tonight.

The company of Liz Harrington, the agent Mike

had told her would arrive, was a far cry from the company of the man she'd fallen in love with—a man who obviously wasn't in love with her.

A wry grimace curved her lips. Mike was a puzzle. She didn't know whether to love him and believe in him, or hate him for toying with her.

Putting him out of her mind meant going back to a life that, while it had its satisfying moments, involved trying to forget an unforgettable man—and his son…a miniature of his father with the same heart-stopping smile.

What a shame, she thought as she went to the kitchen to check on the outdoor lights. Little Jake would have loved to play with Boomer, if only Mike could have forgotten protocol and brought him over. She would have loved watching them play together.

Charlie glanced at her watch and back to the light panel on the wall in the kitchen. She'd ordered an automatic timer, but the red light was glowing. A sure signal that the system was off again.

Staring at the panel, she began to have an uneasy premonition that she would find the locks on the zoo gate broken, too.

After finding the outdoor lights were out, Charlie was afraid to look outside for fear of what she might find. At the same time, she was afraid not to look.

The more apprehensive she became, the more she thought Mike had been telling her the truth, after all. On the other hand, if she were actually in such danger that her life could be at stake, why had he left her for another assignment?

As for Liz Harrington, she hadn't even arrived. Charlie shivered and wished she'd thought to put on heavier clothing. She hadn't wanted Liz's company before, but she knew she'd feel a lot better if Liz was here with her now.

Charlie tried to put her wits together while she prowled the house checking doors and windows.

Would the wires be severed on the outdoor lighting system? Why, and by whom?

Would the lock on the zoo gate be broken for the second time? For what purpose, other than to frighten her?

Hardly, she chided herself, even as her uncomplicated life suddenly became more complicated. Her imagination had to be running away with her. Hadn't she told Mike she was no child and could take care of herself?

She took a flashlight, put on a jacket, put a scarf over her hair and steeled herself to go outside and search the grounds. Most of the animals had seemed to be indifferent about escaping the zoo the last time the gate had been opened, but not little Boomer. If he were loose, she was going to bring the poor little guy into the house to stay with her until all this nonsense was over.

Or was it nonsense?

Charlie slowly made her way down the path leading to the zoo. The padlock was lying on the ground, but luckily none of the animals had noticed. As soon as she reached the small corral where Boomer lived with Lila and two older kangaroos, he bounded out of the darkness and made straight for her.

Charlie laughed and took him into her arms. The little guy was a long way from being a watchdog, but he would make good company for her until Liz Harrington showed up.

She fashioned a tie for the gate out of her scarf and, holding Boomer's paw, started back to the house. A cloud drifted over the moon and, for a few moments before the next cloud shut off moonlight, there was enough light for her to see a car in the driveway leading to the garage. And to see a crumpled figure lying beside it. Liz Harrington?

Charlie dropped Boomer's paw and rushed to investigate.

The figure *was* an unconscious Liz, dressed in the regulation black pantsuit of the Secret Service. There was blood seeping from her hair and a red lump on her forehead. It looked as though she'd been struck by a heavy object and was out cold.

Charlie shuddered. Why Liz? Why now? Had someone mistaken Liz for her? Was someone out to harm her? Had Mike been right when he'd warned her to be careful?

Trained in emergency procedures, she carefully put a finger at the side of Liz's neck. She found a faint pulse, so faint it was hardly discernable. Liz was alive!

Charlie took a deep breath and applied her first-aid training. When she was satisfied the agent was stable, she ran to the house to call 911, Boomer bounding alongside her.

Once inside her house, she rushed to the phone and picked up the receiver. Instead of a reassuring hum, there was only silence. The phone was dead.

She bit back a moan. Whoever had dismantled the lighting system and broken the lock on the gate to the zoo last week had done it again. And this time they'd also cut the telephone wires!

Frantic, Charlie remembered the cell phone she kept in her purse. She ran into her bedroom, grabbed her handbag, called 911 and breathed a sigh of relief.

Boomer, upset by the tension, bounded in circles around Charlie chattering his little heart out.

Charlie knew exactly how he felt. Her heart was pounding so hard she could hear its heavy beat with every breath she took.

While she waited for the 911 personnel to respond to her call, she thought about her experience with Mike. And how close it was to her mother's experience. Mom had alternated between waiting for Dad, an undercover police detective, to come back from an assignment, and waiting to hear he was still alive when he hadn't returned. Until one day her worst fears had been realized.

Charlie had learned early on that to love a lawman was to chance her heart being broken somewhere along the line.

Now there was Mike, a man who professed to care for her. A lawman whose career embodied the same uncertainties and dangers as her late father's.

It didn't make sense that after a lifetime of avoiding men involved with the law, Mike could still make her feel wanted, warm, secure and safe.

Now, tonight, she knew someone out there was watching her. To add to the tension, Liz Harrington, whose only crime had been to try to help her, might die. The only thing that made sense in a world turned upside down for reasons she couldn't reconcile, was the love of the animals she cared for.

Where was Mike when she needed him?

Chapter Eleven

The lights of two police cars responding to Charlie's 911 call lit up the crime scene.

"Sorry ma'am," Sergeant Hawkins of the McLean Police Department showed his badge and introduced himself. He returned Charlie's ID saying, "there's nothing more we can do around here." He gestured to Charlie's pajamas and fuzzy slippers. "I want you to understand you have a choice, but I'm afraid I'll have to ask you to come down to the station. You can wait and come down tomorrow, but it'll be a lot easier for you to remember events if I can debrief you now. Maybe you'd like to get dressed?"

Charlie shivered and crossed her arms, suddenly aware of her thin pajamas. She'd been anxiously watching the ambulance pull away from the house with an unconscious Liz Harrington aboard. Charlie said a little prayer for Liz and forced her attention to the officer. "Let me get this straight. You want me to go down to the police station? For heaven's sake, why? I've told you everything I know!''

Hawkins shrugged. "You say your life is in danger, but it was Miss Harrington who was the victim. There's a discrepancy here. You've got to admit your story is off the wall.''

"I don't know why I'm under attack, and furthermore *I* called you,'' Charlie insisted. Why hadn't Mike given her the whole story? No wonder the police couldn't believe her!

"We always take statements, ma'am. It's routine.''

"Look here, Sergeant Hawkins. I'm an employee of the State Department and I work at Blair House in D.C. Surely, you can take me at my word. The only thing I know is that Liz Harrington, the woman who was attacked, was assigned to protect me.''

"Yeah, well...there *is* a little matter of attempted murder,'' he answered. "And it wasn't yours, Miss Norris.''

His eyebrows rose in a meaningful gesture Charlie read all too well. It was the same look of disbelief Mike used to give her before he got to know her.

She mentally damned Mike for the cloak-and-dagger game he'd involved her in. Not that she doubted she was in danger—not after tonight. "How about the yard lights being disabled? The telephone line being cut? And the broken lock on the gate to the zoo? Not once, but twice? That should tell you something!''

Hawkins glanced up from the notes he was making in his little black notebook. ''Twice? I don't recall seeing any report on the books about another incident.'' He frowned. ''When did the first occurrence take place?''

''Four days ago,'' she said patiently, seething inside but trying not to show it. ''Right after a picnic I hosted for Blair House employees. I guess that at the time I didn't think they were deliberate acts of vandalism.''

''And you didn't see fit to report it?'' Hawkins eyes narrowed. He put the notebook back in his pocket and glared at Boomer. ''Maybe you ought to put that animal back in his cage before we go.''

Charlie didn't like the set look that came over Hawkins's face. And from Boomer's reaction to the tone in the man's voice, neither did the little kangaroo. Either the police sergeant was upset because she hadn't thought the incidents important enough to report, or he believed she was embellishing the facts.

''I can only repeat,'' she said as a cold wind seemed to blow over her. ''The facts speak for themselves. Someone is after me.''

''Why?'' His gaze narrowed even more.

''It's just a feeling I have,'' she answered helplessly, unable to make herself bring Mike and his suspicions into the conversation. She gently patted a shivering Boomer on his back.

"Hey Sarge! You'll never believe what we found back there!"

A hulking uniformed policeman hove into view waving a flashlight and gesturing over his shoulder. Two more policemen followed him. All three were laughing at something they considered funny. After a look at their leader, Charlie had the sinking premonition that Hawkins was in no mood for jokes. "Sergeant…" she began.

Hawkins shot Charlie a stern look to silence her. "Tell me."

"Animals! All kinds! You'd think it was a zoo back there. The only thing missing is a crocodile."

Charlie straightened up. "It *is* a zoo, a private zoo. And before you have anything more to say about it, I have a permit. Not for a crocodile, of course," she hurried to add, "but for the rest of the animals."

Hawkins nodded agreeably. "I know all about the zoo, Miss Norris. I also know the permit limits the number of animals you can keep in there. And that it doesn't give you permission to open the zoo to the public." He paused for effect before he went on. "How much do you charge for admission?"

"Not a penny!"

"Yeah, sure. Do you happen to have an inventory of the animals in your zoo?"

"Yes, as a matter of fact, I do. In the house." Charlie mentally inventoried her pets. The ones she'd purchased, the sick and injured animals people kept asking her to cure, and the animals who wandered in by themselves, like the deer. She didn't want to hazard a guess as to the numbers of the animals currently in the zoo but, with the way her luck was running lately, there were bound to be too many.

She swallowed hard and led the way into the house. From the look of growing determination on Hawkins's face, Charlie had a sinking feeling that, for one reason or another, he was determined to bust her.

As if he sensed Charlie's misgivings, Boomer planted a kiss on her cheek. She nuzzled him back. At a time like this, his support was welcome, but she was rapidly growing aware of something important—she needed a lawyer.

And fast.

"Wait a minute! Am I under arrest?" She glared at Hawkins "If so, I want to call my lawyer."

The sergeant rolled his eyes. She could hear "just like a woman" going through his head. "No, you're not under arrest. I just want to get a few things cleared up, ma'am, but if you'd feel better having a lawyer present while we talk, go right ahead and call one. And by the way," he said as he eyed Boomer, "maybe you'd better get that kangaroo back to his cage before we go."

Boomer swiveled his head and glared at the policeman. Charlie bit her lip. She'd often thought Boomer behaved as if he understood what people were saying, and her suspicion apparently was true. "Boomer doesn't live in a cage. He roams free—in the zoo area, of course. Unless someone breaks the lock on the gate," she added in Boomer's defense. She felt Boomer relax in her arms.

"The kangaroo needs to be secured. Are you going to do it, or shall I?" Hawkins drawled. "If you've decided to come with me, I'd like to get the show on the road."

"I'll go," Charlie answered, actually relieved not to be left home alone. "First, I'll have to call my helper, Freddie, to come over before I can go with you. I can't leave the animals alone."

Hawkins frowned and glanced at his watch. "How long before he gets here?"

"He ought to be here by the time I get dressed. I'll be right back." Charlie hightailed it to the house before Hawkins could stop her.

In her bedroom, she hurriedly called Freddie on her cell phone and asked him to come over right away. Next, she looked through her personal phone book for Dan O'Hara's telephone number. Dan might not be a practicing public lawyer, but at least he knew enough to advise her. Dan could give her any advice she might need to stay out of any more trouble. If she wasn't already in too deep.

AT THIS LATE HOUR of the night, and without its full contingent of policemen and support staff, the police station was dreary and cold. Charlie, bundled up in fleece-lined sweats with a scarf around her neck, felt miserable and disgruntled as she waited for Dan O'Hara to appear. The station's night shift, half asleep or drinking black coffee to stay awake, didn't look too pleased with their lot, either.

Dan O'Hara didn't look any happier than she was feeling when he finally stamped his way into the station.

"You and Mike have the damndest way of getting me involved in things I have no business getting involved in," Dan sighed. "Like I told Mike, I'm supposed to investigate, prosecute or defend navy personnel, not do favors for friends."

"I don't know any private lawyers," Charlie protested. "I've never needed one before!"

"Only by the grace of God, the way I hear it," Dan muttered. "After that shooting in the Blair House, what could you possibly have gotten into now?"

Charlie glared at him.

Hawkins leaned forward in his swivel chair. He'd tried to look busy, but Charlie knew he'd been watching her like a hawk. "What's this about a shooting incident?"

O'Hara waved him off. "Take it from me, you don't want to know. Besides, the incident didn't happen in your jurisdiction."

"Maybe so," Hawkins said, "but a shooting involving Miss Norris sure gives me a broader picture of what the lady could be involved in."

Charlie bristled. Everyone, including Dan from the few words he'd let drop, seemed to know more about what was going on than she did. "If you know what all this is about, how about sharing that information with me?"

Hawkins ignored her. He glanced down at the zoo inventory in front of him and soberly eyed Charlie. "I'm afraid I'm going to have to cite you for keeping more animals on your property than your permit allows."

Bewildered, Charlie eyed the sergeant. She'd not only expected more questions about the shooting, she was beginning to suspect bringing her down to the station over the number of animals she had in her zoo had only been a pretext to hide the truth. As far as she was concerned, Hawkins thought he was investigating a murder. "You know just by looking at the list?"

"Yep. For instance, you have three horses?"

"Temporarily," Charlie hurried to add. "I'm taking care of them for a friend."

Hawkins sighed and pulled his citation book out of his desk drawer. "The law in this county says you're allowed one horse. As for the rest of the animals on your list, I'll have to check them out with the animal regulation people to see if they're legal."

Charlie turned to O'Hara. "Do something!"

Dan shrugged. "Like I said, I'm a navy lawyer. I suggest you pay the fine and let me take you home."

Charlie was about to protest when a warning look passed over O'Hara's face. She shut her mouth. Dan obviously knew more than he was willing to admit or she was a monkey's aunt.

"Here you go." Hawkins handed her the citation. "By the way, don't leave town."

Feeling like a criminal, Charlie accepted the citation and headed for the station door.

Dan exchanged a few words with Hawkins, shook the man's hand and followed Charlie. "I'll take you home and check out the yard lights for you. Maybe I can get them working. In the meantime, if it'll make you feel any better, my next advice to you is to cool it for now. Mike told me he's working on the problem."

"What *is* the problem?" Charlie burst out, more frustrated than ever. "Mike's only hinted around it."

Dan shook his head. "That's for him to tell you.

But, I have a strong feeling the danger will be over soon.''

When they pulled up to Charlie's house, Freddie, flashlight in hand, rushed out to meet them. ''Charlie! I've been trying to reach you. Boomer's gone!''

Charlie's heart skipped. Boomer would never have run away by himself. He was so young and helpless, barely out of diapers. Either someone had stolen him or he had to be out there somewhere looking for her. Who was taking care of him? Who was making sure he wouldn't get killed on some highway?

Hawkins was out on a call when she used her cell phone to call the police station and report Boomer missing. When she told his assistant Boomer was gone, the man couldn't stop laughing. ''How can a kangaroo get lost, lady?''

''Forget it, I'll take care of it myself.'' Charlie jammed the phone back in her purse and rushed out to her car. ''You stay here and keep an eye on the rest of the animals,'' she called to Freddie. ''If Boomer is anywhere out there alone and frightened, I'll find him.''

HIS BRIEF ASSIGNMENT over, Mike checked in to Blair House Monday morning and asked to speak to Liz Harrington.

''She hasn't checked in this morning, Mike,'' his

secretary, Dina, said. "I heard she's in the hospital, D.C. General, I think."

Mike swore. Warning bells sounded, and they weren't ringing only for Liz. "What happened? How's she doing?"

"Nobody's saying, but I hear she's going to be okay. I'm worried about her."

Mike rubbed his aching forehead. A brass band was playing kettledrums on top of his head. "How about Charlie Norris?"

"She hasn't come in yet, either. Want me to page her on her cell phone?"

"No, thanks. She's probably at home. I'll look her up myself." He hadn't told anyone Liz had offered to keep an extra-close eye on Charlie for him, but he was damn well sure whatever had happened last night had something to do with Charlie. More to the point, he had to find out if Charlie was there in the hospital with her. He checked his watch with a frown. The warning bells were ringing louder. Something wasn't right.

"By the way, Dina, please leave a message to Simons from me. Tell him I checked in and that I'm taking a personal day."

"Just like that?"

"Yeah. Just like that," Mike hung up before his secretary could protest. Cussing his bad luck for leaving Charlie alone, he headed for her house.

From now on, he vowed, he wasn't going to let Charlie out of his sight.

As he drove to McLean, he grimly thought of what he wanted to do with Charlie when he found her. To her and for her. This time, he promised himself, he wasn't going to stop with a kiss. And when he was through showing her how much she meant to him, she'd know they damn well belonged together.

He was through pussyfooting around. The next time he saw Charlie, he was going to show her how much he loved her, find out if she loved him.

As he drove through the early-morning traffic, he mulled over how he did feel about Charlie. In the two long days away from her, he'd realized how much he missed her, her smile, her touch, her fascinating approach to life and, yes, even that quirky kangaroo of hers who seemed to think he was a human baby.

First things first. He needed to visit Liz to see if there was anything he could do for her and to find out if Charlie was with her.

After visiting Liz, he promised himself, he'd set out to find the bastard who'd threatened Charlie and who had hurt Liz.

The special cell phone he kept in his pocket rang. It was the smaller of the two cell phones he carried. It could be folded to look like a pocket calendar. At the sound, a shiver ran over him. Only three contacts knew this private telephone number; his mother, the State Department, and, for the past week, Dan O'Hara.

"Wheeler here."

"O'Hara. Meet me at the coffee shop."

Mike's heart leapt in his chest. O'Hara would never have called if he weren't on to something vitally important. "Got something?"

"Maybe. I'll tell you when I see you."

Mike thought of Charlie at home, perhaps waiting for him. "Does it have to be now?"

"The sooner the better. The commander's back in town."

"Tell him I'll be in touch after I see Charlie."

"About that…"

The hair stood up on Mike's neck. "Something wrong? I've already heard about Liz. What about Charlie? Is she okay?"

"You might say so. At least she was when I left her."

"Left her?" Mike was beyond feeling anxious. The dramatic tone in O'Hara's voice spelled trouble of the worst kind. "Spill it!"

Mike heard O'Hara sigh, people's usual reaction whenever Charlie's name was mentioned. "Damn it, O'Hara! What's going on?"

"Okay, but I don't think you're going to like it." O'Hara filled him in on the attempt on Liz Harrington's life, the inoperative yard lights, the open zoo gate and the cut telephone wires.

"And you left Charlie alone after all that?"

"Not before I checked out the premises. Charlie seemed okay with it."

Mike cussed until he ran out of breath. "Tell the commander I'll get in touch with him after I make sure Charlie is unharmed. Got it?"

"Got it."

Mike floored the foot pedal.

He breathed more easily when he reached Charlie's house and the premises looked normal. He rang the doorbell, then knocked on the door.

No response.

His heart pounding, Mike ran around to the back of the house and checked the back door and knocked again. When there was still no answer, he stepped back, hunched his shoulder and broke in the door. A quick check in and around the house told him Charlie wasn't home and her car was missing. What really bothered him was that with Liz Harrington in the hospital Charlie was out there alone somewhere.

The zoo! Mike raced to the zoo. Charlie's red scarf tied the gates closed. Evidence that O'Hara's story of what had gone on last night hadn't been a fairy tale.

Except that O'Hara had told him he'd driven Charlie home from the police station. Why had she taken off? Where had she gone?

He had to find her. And now!

Mike drove around the surrounding country roads looking for Charlie's car. He was about to give up when he saw her bright red Toyota parked in front of a small convenience store.

Swearing a blue streak, he strode into the store to find Charlie in jeans and a heavy sweatshirt posting a notice on a community bulletin board.

"Charlie!" When she turned at the sound of his voice, he realized that, in his relief, he'd frightened her. "I'm sorry, sweetheart. I didn't mean to sound like an ass. It's just that I've been so worried about you. Dan told me what happened. Are you all right?"

"All right? You get me involved in some kind of cloak-and-dagger operation without telling me what it is! You disappear after leaving me a vague e-mail message! You let me worry about you and expect me to be all right with it?" She looked as if she wanted to take a swing at him.

"I couldn't tell you, sweetheart. I'm sorry, but it's part of my job." He squirmed under the baleful look she shot him. If looks could kill, he would have been a dead man by now. "Come on, give me a break. I'd tell you the whole story if I could."

Charlie stared at him, her expression torn. "I think I ought to know the facts if they involve me. Maybe I could have avoided some of the problems."

Mike nodded. "You're right. I'll try to do better."

He looked at her disheveled hair, the fleece sweat-shirt and the dark circles under her eyes. He wanted to take her in his arms to comfort her. He couldn't. The last thing he needed was for Charlie to fall apart.

"O'Hara told me what happened to Liz, even about the vandalism to the lights and the zoo. At least Liz is in the hospital being taken care of." His gaze swept her. "How about you?"

"I'm fine," she finally muttered, "but I don't think the rest of the world is doing too well. Not with all the crazies out there."

He winced at the angry look in Charlie's eyes. "You're sure?"

"I'm sure." She turned back to the bulletin board and, muttering under breath, angrily stuck another pin in the bulletin board.

Mike glanced over her shoulder at the index card she was pinning to the board. "What's that for?"

Charlie swore under her breath as she pricked her finger with a tack. She sucked a tiny drop of blood that welled up on the ball of her forefinger. "Boomer is missing. I've looked everywhere for him with no luck. I'm hoping that whoever has found him will see this card and will call me."

Mike put an arm around her shoulders. He wanted to kiss her wounded finger, but he sensed it wasn't the time. Instead, he'd let her focus on Boomer. Knowing how much she cared for the little animal, he wasn't surprised to find her shaking with anger. "Did you check at the police station?"

Charlie sniffed. "Police station! They're not much better than you are. The sergeant is already convinced I'm a nutcase. When I told his assistant Boomer was missing, the guy couldn't stop laughing. He told me he had something more important to take care of and that Boomer would come home when he was good and ready."

Mike eyed a fuming Charlie. He didn't blame her for being upset. To his way of thinking the folks down at the McLean Police Department needed an attitude adjustment. As for Charlie, the angrier she became, he had a feeling, the less likely the possibility that she would fall apart. "Boomer would never run away. Not from you," he added, remembering how fond the little marsupial was of Charlie. He recalled how the little guy evidently thought she was his mother, and, heaven forbid, would make Mike his father. He smothered a smile.

He led Charlie to the door. "Let's go home, sweetheart. You can leave your car there, and we'll take mine to search for Boomer. Maybe we can come up with some fresh ideas. Boomer can't be too far away. We'll find him."

Mike followed Charlie home and waited for her to park her car and to come back to join him. "Tell me where you've already looked," he said, setting the car in motion. "We'll take it from there."

Two hours later, after an empty search and a quick lunch at the nearest fast-food restaurant, he finally headed back to Charlie's. "Let's go home. Maybe Boomer's come back."

Charlie's red Toyota was still there, but its tires were slashed and its windshield shattered.

Mike reached for Charlie before she had a chance to open the car door. "Wait up! Let me check things out!"

He rounded the car and checked for a possible armed booby trap. Come hell or high water, he swore silently, he was never going to leave Charlie alone again. Not until he found the person who had sent those threatening letters. No matter how Charlie might feel about having him around at night.

"Come on inside," he told a shaking Charlie. "I want to report this."

"Maybe now someone will *have* to believe me," she muttered.

Mike nodded. If only he would be allowed to provide the proof. Soon.

After making the telephone call, he followed Charlie into her bedroom. "Charlie?"

She stopped in the process of pulling the sweatshirt over her head. With her arms uplifted, her jeans slipped below her waist. He could see the edge of a pale pink lacy bra and a matching thong. "What?"

"Come here."

He'd already fantasized about what he'd do with

Charlie when he caught up with her. Now, he intended to make some of the fantasies come true—for both of them.

No dummy, Charlie's eyes grew wary. "Why? You're only going to leave again, aren't you?"

"I may have to, but not just yet. First, I want you to do something for me."

"What?" She froze in place, the sweatshirt held against her breasts.

"Stop talking and come here." Mike hadn't meant to be so obvious, but it was the only way he knew to answer the question in her eyes.

He told himself he was here because he couldn't leave Charlie alone to wonder when someone out there would harm her. It was more than that. He wanted Charlie more than he'd wanted anything or anyone in his life.

All the things he'd planned to take care of today: visit Liz and ask her if she could identify her assailant, talk to Stevens and get a lead or two, faded from his mind as he gazed at Charlie's lovely figure. He knew one thing for certain. He was not only going to stay, he intended to do his best to satisfy the longing he saw in Charlie's eyes. And satisfy his desire for her at the same time.

If ever there was a time to show Charlie how he cared for her, this was it. "Come here," he repeated, his arms held out to her.

To his relief, Charlie finally nodded and slowly

moved into his arms. "Just for a moment," she said and shivered. "And only because I'm so cold."

"I know," he said softly. He drew her lips to meet his own. "Let me warm you," he said and kissed her with all the passion pent up in him.

"If you insist," she said with a shy smile. "I always try my best to do what you ask."

"I wish," Mike muttered, sensing Charlie was trying to cover her uncertainty about how he felt about her. No problem. Before they were through, she was going to find he was more serious than he'd ever been in his life. She'd *know* what he had already discovered—they belonged together. "Ready?"

Chapter Twelve

Charlie blushed under Mike's heated touch. His hands were warm on her skin; his smile blatantly sensuous. She'd already decided to make love to him with all the passion she had in her, but nothing had prepared her for the smoldering look in his eyes.

She put her arms around his neck and opened her mouth to give him entry. She was grateful for Mike's arms, his warmth, but it wasn't his comfort she longed for—she wanted *him*. Wanted him to hold her, bare skin sliding against bare skin. She wanted his hands to caress her throbbing breasts, to ease the growing ache in her middle. To feel him all around her, over her and inside her.

When Mike crushed her to him, Charlie sensed he wanted more of her, too. She tugged at his jacket, slid it off his shoulders and stood back to admire his broad shoulders, the way his shirt strained against his masculine chest.

Next, she undid his black tie and tossed it aside.

"You won't be needing that," she murmured, "or this." She unbuttoned his shirt, one white button at a time. Next she drew his undershirt over his head and uncovered the inviting mat of tangled dark brown hair. She ran her fingers through the curls, reveling in the warmth of his skin and the way his eyes darkened. She felt her temperature rise, her breasts harden and an ache grow deep in her middle.

His belt buckle was next. As she struggled to unfasten it, she eyed the dark curls that formed a path to his waist, disappearing below the black leather belt. Her fingers itched to slide below his belt, touch him in the same way she wanted him to touch her.

"I'm not sure about this," she said, her voice shaking, when her fingers couldn't behave. "The only male I ever undressed was my brother, and he was only three years old."

Mike smiled his satisfaction. "For a novice, you're doing great!"

"Only great?" Her hands paused.

"More than great," he said succinctly, his gaze challenging her to continue.

The buckle then his zipper came undone. Charlie slowly gathered the waist of his pants and slid them down his legs. Certain that his long, muscled legs would soon be wrapped around her, she dropped her shaking hands and stood back. "Maybe you ought to continue from here."

His gaze locked with hers, a wry smile on his

face. "If you insist," he said and stepped out of the garment that had fallen to his ankles. "Now what, sweetheart?"

"Love me, just love me," she said again, going back into his arms. She clung to him, so close a leaf wouldn't have had room to get between them.

"There's only one way I know how to do that," Mike laughed softly. He drew her hair away from the nape of her neck and gently kissed her on a sensitive spot. "But only if you're sure you want me to."

Want him? She wanted him with every inch of her body, with every breath she took. "You're driving me out of my mind. Can't you tell?" She'd been right about Mike—beneath his strong persona, there lurked a gentle man.

How could she tell him she didn't want gentle? She wanted to come alive in his arms, to forget all the reasons she'd thought of for not saying yes.

She intended to shut out the world, forget the past and the future. To remember only that this was Mike. A man she'd grown to love and who held her in his arms as if he loved her, too.

"You still have too many clothes on," he whispered. He rubbed her bare shoulders and kissed the dimples on the back of her shoulders. When he reached around her and undid her bra, her breasts crushed against his chest. She gasped at the sharp yet sweet sensation that ran through her.

"Sorry, something wrong?"

"No. Something's very right." Suddenly shy, Charlie smiled into Mike's eyes. This was the moment she'd been hoping for. The moment when she could show him how much she cared for him. And, if there was a lucky star in the heavens shining down on her, to find he cared for her, too.

Mike ran his hands over her shoulders and down to her waist. Just when she felt as if her knees had turned to rubber, he paused, his hands at the zipper of her jeans. "You want to do the rest, sweetheart, or shall I?"

"Together," she said with a catch in her breath.

"Wise woman." Mike gathered her in his arms and rewarded her with another kiss.

The kiss was only the beginning. She stroked his back, relishing the warm skin, the flow of his muscles and laughed for the sheer joy of the moment.

Mike froze. "What?"

"Nothing, I'm just happy," she said and swallowed a sigh of pleasure.

He murmured his own pleasure as he stroked her thighs with a slow, deep sensuous rhythm that made her squirm with pleasure. "I don't think I can wait much longer."

"Neither can I," she whispered. He pulled her closer. So close she felt his hard response against her hip.

"I want you. No more waiting. I warn you, I intend to be thorough." His voice faded as he lowered his head to tongue her breasts.

Thorough. Charlie's insides were churning with anticipation.

"Touch me, sweetheart," he said softly. "See what you do to me."

Charlie caressed his strong arms and his muscled chest. She felt the muscles there tighten under her hand, and his nipples harden. She pulled back when she heard him catch his breath.

"I didn't know men reacted like that," she said, gazing in wonder at the change in him. "I thought that only happened to women."

"You're in for a lot of surprises," he said with a shaky laugh as he pulled her close. "We're as human as you are."

"Your turn," Charlie finally said when she couldn't take any more of the sensuous way his hands swept down her back to her hips, her thighs, or of his arousal brushing against her. Every inch of her yearned to belong to Mike, the first man to whom she'd given her heart and her soul.

Mike smiled down at her. "Come on, sweetheart," he said. He led her to the waiting bed and fell on it with her in his arms. When she gasped in surprise, he flipped them over, supporting his weight above her with his arms. He smiled down at her.

"Warmer, now?" he whispered as he ran his fingers through her hair, gently tucking it behind her ears, and kissed the hollow between her breasts.

Charlie closed her eyes and let herself sink in a sea of almost overwhelming sensation. "Burning."

"Good." He dropped feathery kisses on her middle and moved south. South, until she thought she couldn't take it without melting into a puddle of molten need.

She wove her fingers in his hair and pulled him back up to where she could kiss him. "Sure of yourself, aren't you?"

He smiled knowingly and positioned himself between her legs. "Can't miss when you're the woman I'm making love to."

"Love?"

"Mmm…don't you ever doubt it." He nibbled on her taut breasts, reached to caress that part of her that would surely turn her into a bonfire. She moaned. As if it were a signal, he kissed her and slid into her warmth. She met his thrusts with her own, her wanton emotions spiraling higher and higher until they burst over her like a Fourth of July fireworks display. Seconds later, she heard Mike's shout as he reached his own pleasure.

Charlie cuddled into Mike's warmth and heard him whisper. "Are you all right, sweetheart?"

All right? Her face hidden, Charlie smiled into Mike's damp and heated chest. He'd turned her world on its axis and made her feel as if she'd been tossed in a stormy, restless sea. Even now, images of shooting stars, a rainbow of brilliant colors lingered behind her closed eyes.

Part of her was thrilled to hear Mike say he loved her. Another part of her asked what good his love was if he kept passing in and out of her life?

She didn't want to know the answer. Not now. And, maybe never. Not when she was held in Mike's arms, his warm, reassuring breath against her cheek. She'd spend tonight in his arms, tomorrow would have to take care of itself.

She drew in deep breaths of Mike's male scent and turned her thoughts to the moment. "Mike?"

"Mmm?" he muttered sleepily from where he lay across her breasts.

"I think I'm falling in love with you."

That was enough to awaken Mike. He hid a smile and debated making love to Charlie again, to show just how thorough he could be, but she was slipping into sleep. He grunted a vague reply and pulled her into his arms. Cuddled into his warmth, he heard her ask, "Stay with me tonight?"

He kissed her closed eyes. "I promise."

Mike lay awake long after Charlie had fallen asleep in his arms. Oddly enough, she tasted of oranges and peanut butter. An incongruous combination, but what was Charlie if not a mixture of incongruous personalities?

But irresponsible?

How had he ever thought of Charlie as irresponsible? No way. She was probably the most responsible person he knew. If it came to that, he'd trust her with his life, he thought as he inhaled her sweet scent. God willing, he wouldn't have to. It was her life he was trying to protect.

At work, she treated VIP guests at Blair House as if they were guests in her home. She took in and cared for animals other people had discarded or who needed her care. And she even treated Boomer as if he were a child of hers.

She was also the most vital person he'd ever known.

He was through trying to change her.

In the early hours of the morning, when Charlie awakened, her body still tingled from the memory of the touch of Mike's hands stroking her body. She touched her lips, lips swollen from deep kisses, and smiled. Pleased with the memories, she stretched and turned over to reach for him. He was gone.

Together with a rose covered with morning dew, Charlie found a note on her pillow: "Had to leave. Back later," it said. To add to her worry, he gave no reason for his departure.

Charlie shrank back into the pillows that were still warm from Mike's body and that still carried his scent. After promising to stay with her, why hadn't he awakened her and explained where he was going and when he expected to return? She might not have asked him to stay, but at least she would know where he was going and why.

Just as she'd breathlessly waited as a child for her father to return from some special assignment, it was her turn to wait for the man she loved. And to pray he would return unhurt.

MIKE DROVE back to D.C., his thoughts on the sweet smile that had curved Charlie's lips as she slept. Rather than awakening her from what must have been a pleasant dream, he'd gone out to her garden and picked the most beautiful red rose he could find. He'd almost chosen a yellow rose for remembrance, but, under the circumstances, a red rose pledging love had seemed more fitting.

Charlie might not know the meaning of the floral language of love, he thought dryly, but he did. Oddly enough, it had been one of the few things his late wife had taught him. Too bad she hadn't taken the legend to heart.

He slid his car into a parking place marked U.S. Government and strode down the street and into the coffeehouse where, in response to his telephone call, he and O'Hara had agreed to meet. But not before he swept the room for any sign of something or someone suspicious.

Dan rose and motioned to Mike. "How's Charlie? The local gendarmes sure gave her a bad time the other night, poor kid."

"Great. Sleeping when I left her. As for the local law, I intend to have a talk with them." He eyed O'Hara's immaculate navy-blue uniform. "On duty today?"

O'Hara slapped Mike on the back. "I'm glad to see you and Charlie have finally become friends. And yes, I am."

Friends? Mike smothered his response at the thought of the passion he'd discovered lurking in Charlie last night. And at the memory of damp entangled limbs and heated kisses. And of years of loving still to come.

"You'll be okay as soon as you have a cup of coffee," O'Hara said with a knowing laugh at Mike's introspective silence. "Let's get on with this. I'm buying this time. I've got to get back to JAG headquarters before they discover I'm missing."

"And I've got to get back before Charlie wakes up." Mike dropped into his chair. "What have you found out?"

Dan sipped his coffee, glared at his Danish and pushed it aside. "God, how I hate being a middle man," he muttered. "I just hope the JAG is understanding, or I'm going to be raked over hot coals by my ears. I'd hate to mess with the Judge Advocate General of the navy."

"I've met the admiral. Underneath all that tough image, Crowley is probably a softie." Mike reached for the Danish, an almond bear claw. "I'm starved. I didn't stop for breakfast."

"Enjoy." Dan shifted in his chair. "Just remember this is between Stevens, me and you. The last thing the commander wants is to start a diplomatic brouhaha."

"Got it." Mike bit into the Danish.

"Wade ran a check on the men and women assigned to Baronovia's new embassy opening here in D.C. next week. Most of the staff is still in Europe, but a few advance members are here to hire local help."

"And?"

"Wade came up with two likely suspects. Nothing concrete, you understand," O'Hara hurried to add, "but still possible suspects."

Danish forgotten, Mike leaned over the table. "Get to it, man!"

"One is a Caspar Schmitz. He's heading up the security liaison between Baronovia and the U.S. Fairly new at the game, Wade said, but it seems he's some VIP's grandson."

Mike's eyebrows rose. Security measures and their implementation were in his blood and he'd spent many years working at it. How could an inexperienced operator be given a position so important? "And they trust him with such an important job?"

O'Hara shrugged. "Seems Prince Alexis owed his grandfather."

Mike shuddered. "Thank God it's the marines who handle security at our embassies. Who else?" Mike eyed Dan impatiently. As far as he was concerned, things were coming up empty.

"Irine Baron. A distant cousin."

"A woman?"

"Yeah. Wade suspects she's from the wrong side of the blanket. Still she's considered a member of the Baron family. She's in charge of the local office hiring."

"Is she a local?"

"Not that I know of."

"So how does she know enough of what goes on around here to staff an embassy?"

O'Hara shrugged again. "Like I told you, I know zilch about the business. I'll leave that up to you. Me, I'm just a navy lawyer."

Mike digested the skeletal information. "It doesn't sound as if either one is the type to harass Charlie. What would they have to gain?"

O'Hara shrugged. "You can ask Wade that question when he gets here this weekend. He must have some ideas, but he told me he couldn't say anything more just now."

"Maybe he intends to let the culprit hang himself—or herself. I just don't have time to wait around until it happens." Mike stared into the mirror that hung above the serving counter, imagined he saw Charlie's face in it and stood. "I'm off to D.C. General Hospital. I want to look in on Liz Harrington and see if she needs anything. Maybe she can shed some light on who attacked her."

"Stay cool," O'Hara warned. "Give the lady my best. And don't forget to keep an eye on Charlie."

Mike grinned sheepishly. "You don't have to remind me. I'm through hiding anything from my lady. From now on, we're in this together."

CHARLIE WAS PACING the kitchen floor, a tepid cup of coffee in her hands when Mike knocked. She tried to hide the feeling of relief that swept her. She opened the back door. "Come in. You don't have to knock. Not after last night."

Mike closed the door behind him. He wanted to take her in his arms and pick up where they'd left off early this morning, but first things first.

"You're wrong there, Charlie Norris!" He took two steps forward. At the tone in his voice and his use of her full name, she took two careful steps back. "The only way to know who's on the other side of the door is to keep the doors and windows locked and to have the caller identify himself," he went on. "Do I make myself clear?"

"Ahh, of course—the security lecture," she said. She strode to the sink, poured out the cold coffee and glared at him. "Don't you ever think of anything else?"

"Damn right I do," he said, catching her by her arm and turning her around to face him. "I think of you. All the time. And as far as I can see, you're your own worst enemy." He went on to read her chapter and verse of what had happened and what she could have done to avoid it.

Charlie froze in his arms. All she heard of the rest of his lecture was that he thought of her…all the time. "You really care for me?"

"Damn right I do," he repeated carefully. "In fact, I think I love you." He paused and pulled her into his arms. "Scratch that. I *know* I love you." He laughed as if the discovery was a joke on him. "How does that sound?"

"Lovely." Charlie smiled into his eyes, her anger dissolved in a rush of affection. "I love you, too. Care to have me show you how much?"

"Oh, yeah!" he muttered into her lips. "Only not just now. I have to go check on Liz."

Liz! Charlie felt guilty. How could she have forgotten the woman who might have taken a blow meant for her? "I'll go with you." She paused. "If it's okay with you?"

"Right," Mike grinned. "Since I can't seem to trust you to follow my advice, I wouldn't dream of leaving home without you."

LIZ HARRINGTON lay back against a nest of pillows. An IV line was attached to one wrist, she had a black eye, her head was bandaged and one foot covered with a cast rested in a sling. Mike had had a bouquet of flowers delivered but an antiseptic odor lingered in the air.

"No problem," she said after Charlie had apologized for the beating. "It's all in the line of duty."

"I doubt Simons will believe that," Mike said dryly. "You were doing me a favor, and on your own time. It's me he's going to chew out."

Liz shrugged and turned her gaze on Charlie. "Funny thing, you and I don't even look alike. Why would anyone go after me?"

Why indeed? Mike turned a thoughtful gaze on Liz. Something she'd said rang a bell. "You didn't happen to witness the shooting in Blair House last week, did you?"

Liz thought back. "I was on vacation at the time, but I'd come back in to get something out of the office."

"And?"

"I remember now." She stared at Mike. "A man rushed out of Blair and almost knocked me over. He apologized as he ran, but I still think he was an ass for barreling out that way."

Charlie stared at Liz. "You saw him?"

Liz put a hand to her forehead. "I think so. Tall, thin, mustached. Uniform?"

Charlie slowly nodded. ''I didn't have a clear picture of him in my mind until you described him, but I remember now. You're right.''

Mike broke in. ''Foreign accent?''

Liz nodded.

Mike swore under his breath. Why hadn't he gone through a more thorough investigation after the shooting? Liz might not be lying there in bed, and he wouldn't have had to worry about Charlie. ''That makes two of you who are in danger,'' he said thoughtfully. He reached for the phone. ''I'll arrange for around-the-clock surveillance of your room, Liz. If anything out of the ordinary happens, ring or call for help.''

He grabbed Charlie. ''And as for you, I'm not going to let you out of my sight. Let's go.''

''Where to?''

''We're off to see the duchess,'' Mike answered with a grin. ''Together.''

A QUICK PHONE CALL revealed that May was once again a guest in Blair House. And with her, courtesy of the State Department and the Under Secretary of the Navy, was her husband, JAG Commander Wade Stevens.

The duchess ran to embrace Charlie. ''Charlie! Charlie Norris! What fun to finally see you again! I was hoping you would be here when we arrived.''

Charlie hugged her back. "I'm afraid I was involved in something important, Your Grace."

"Call me May." The duchess smiled happily. "I'm Mrs. Wade Stevens now, remember?"

Charlie remembered the wedding and the two days of festivities that had preceded it all too well. It had been a romantic period, but had also been the first time the jinx of falling over Mike had first struck.

She held out a hand and motioned for Mike to join them. "You remember Mike Wheeler, your Secret Service bodyguard when you were last here, don't you?"

May held out her hand. "I certainly do. Are you still trying to keep Charlie and me out of trouble, Mr. Wheeler?"

"Not with much success, I'm afraid." Mike traded ironic glances with Wade Stevens, resplendent in his navy-blue uniform. "Commander?"

Wade shrugged at Mike's unspoken suggestion they adjourn to share information. "Might as well talk right here. My wife insists."

"I do," May agreed. "I am sure I can help. Come, we can use the library to talk."

Charlie hung back long enough to order pastries, tea for May and coffee for everyone else.

Once the doors were closed behind them, Wade Stevens wasted no time. "Better start at the beginning, Mike."

Mike hesitated and glanced at Charlie.

"It's about time," Charlie frowned at Mike. "Now, maybe *I'll* learn what this is all about."

"It's not for publication, understood?" Mike's glance encompassed the other three.

"You mean Charlie doesn't know?" May cast a reproachful look at Mike. "I understood the problem concerned her."

Mike spoke up. "It did, and it does. Unfortunately, I wasn't allowed to give Charlie all the details. But after what's been happening…" He went on to reveal the threatening letters, the plan to use Charlie as a decoy and the subsequent events.

Charlie shuddered. Mike put his arm around her shoulders. "Everything's going to be okay, sweetheart."

May's eyebrows rose at the endearment. "At least something good has come out of this problem."

Mike felt embarrassed. "Yeah. You could say so."

"And you think my country is somehow involved in all of this?"

"Sorry, yes." Mike hesitated, then went on. "But the two possible suspects your husband came up with just don't fit the picture of someone against the opening of Baronovia's new embassy."

Wade agreed. "It has to be someone from the old trade office. Someone who has a lot to lose when that office closes down."

"Got a name?"

"Gregor Petrov," May interjected softly. "He is the head of Baronovia's trade office until our embassy opens here."

"Got an address to go with the name?"

"An office building off Columbus Square. Wait a minute and I'll give it to you." Wade strode to the desk, dug in a drawer for paper and pen and wrote down the address for Mike.

Alarmed, Charlie grabbed Mike's arm. "Wait a minute! You don't intend to take on this Petrov by yourself, do you?"

He nodded grimly. "I sure don't intend to go through channels. I can get the job done faster by myself." He paused, frustrated. "Damn it, even if he's the perp, we still have a problem."

"What kind of problem?" Wade set his coffee cup down on the table and glanced at May. "Off the record, but can we help?"

"No. We've been through this before—even if we get Petrov, he'll get away with attempted murder. As a member of Baronovia's diplomatic staff, he's able to claim diplomatic immunity."

"Not anymore!" May Stevens set her teacup on the table so hard the china rattled. Before everyone's eyes, she turned into the duchess Mary Louise, second in line to the throne of Baronovia. "You prove the man guilty, and I'll see to his dismissal and return to Baronovia for prosecution. Immediately!"

Chapter Thirteen

Mike congratulated himself as he headed to Charlie's place. He was almost home free. With the duchess on his side and Charlie safely stashed at home, he had nothing to worry about, except finding the man who was threatening Charlie.

Beside him, Charlie seemed so deep in thought she didn't notice he was headed across the Beltway to McLean, until a familiar highway sign shocked her out of her reverie. "Where are we going?"

"Home."

"Home?" She looked out the window at the passing landscape and finally noticed they were headed out of D.C. "I thought we were going to look for Petrov?"

"*I* am. *You're* going home."

"Over my dead body," Charlie declared. She twisted in her seat belt to stare at him. "Turn this car around."

"Your death is exactly what I'm trying to prevent, sweetheart," Mike replied in an effort to placate her. From the grim expression on her face, it wasn't working. "Besides, I thought you wanted to go home to look for Boomer."

Charlie didn't look pleased. She glared at him. "Stop treating me like a child, Mike. Besides Liz, I'm the only one who can identify the second shooter, and you know it. As for Boomer, Freddie is out looking for him as we speak. Now, do what I said, turn this car around."

Mike kept driving while Charlie kept up a steady stream of reasons why she should be included in the coming action.

Treat Charlie like a child! If she hadn't sounded so serious, he would have been tempted to laugh. Mentally and physically, Charlie was not only light-years away from being a child, she was the most fascinating and exciting woman he'd ever met. With her tossed blond hair, flashing blue eyes and flushed cheeks, she was also one of the most beautiful. No way was he going to put her in harm's way if he could help it. And he could. If there was going to be a dead body, it was going to be Petrov's.

"...and that's why I still think I should go with you!"

"No," Mike said firmly. He kept his eyes on the road, but his right ear was burning.

Charlie fumed.

"It's my life we're talking about here, you know."

"Damn right." Mike focused on keeping his cool as he turned off the highway and narrowly missed a car coming in the other direction. The driver swerved and sounded his horn, but not before making an obscene gesture through the open car window.

"Road rage. What happened to 'have a great day'?" Mike muttered. He glanced over at his visibly disgruntled companion. "I'm serious, Charlie. I want you to stay home until I get back."

She stared at him sourly. "Just how far do you think I can go without a car?"

Belatedly, Mike remembered Charlie's car had been vandalized. He smiled wryly at the futility of trying to keep a woman like Charlie pinned down, but the lack of a car was a good place to start.

He turned into Charlie's driveway, glided to a halt at her back door and turned off the ignition. While she watched, he dropped the car keys into the inside pocket of his jacket. Just in case she decided to wrestle him for them. "Out, please."

Charlie's eyes narrowed. "You don't trust me, do you?"

"With my life," he answered, gesturing to the car door. "But not with yours."

Before Charlie could let loose with another blast of outrage, he slid out of the car and tugged her after him. Once outside, he set her on her feet, raised his eyebrows and smiled down at her. "Charlie, my love, I have a strong feeling the only way I can be sure you'll stay put is to handcuff you to your bed."

Her eyes widened in shock. "You wouldn't!"

Mike smiled and gently brushed her cheek with his knuckles. "No, sweetheart. It was just a fleeting thought. But come to think of it," he added as he enfolded her in his arms and lowered his lips to hers, "it *would* make for some interesting foreplay."

Charlie blinked when Mike touched his tongue to hers and deepened his kiss. Thoughts of romantic foreplay sent electric shocks coursing through her. Making love with him last night had been thorough, satisfying and thrilling, but handcuffs?

Dismayed, yet enthralled, she felt her body warm as she pictured them in bed together playing sexual games. If this was the same Mike Wheeler who'd lived by and with the Secret Service manual as his bible, he had certainly changed. And, somehow, without her knowing it, he had managed to change her in the process. From a woman who had avoided romantic entanglements for fear of losing the man she loved, she was plunging head over heels in love with Mike.

But not enough to make her forget that men who lived by the gun risked dying by the gun.

She clutched Mike's jacket and rested her head against his chest. She heard his heart beating heavily, echoing the wild beat of her own heart. As surely as she belonged to him, he belonged to her, she mused happily.

Mike thought he'd won the argument, but she had other plans for him tonight. She wasn't about to lose the love of her life now—not for all the international crazies out there. The duchess and her husband could take care of Petrov and his kind. She intended to take care of her own.

She smoothed Mike's jacket lapels, fingered the buttons on his jacket and slowly worked her fingers inside his shirt. "Stay with me tonight?" She made small circles on his heated skin as she spoke.

He muttered something under his breath before he buried his face in her hair and ran his thumbs up the sides of her throat. "I wish."

"You can," she whispered. "No one knows about our meeting with Wade and May this afternoon but Dan O'Hara. Let's forget it. If the man who wrote the threatening letters turns out to be a Baronovian national, why not let May and Wade take care of him? For my sake?"

Mike shook his head. With one last, deep kiss that sent shock waves rushing all the way down to her toes, he absently caressed her cheek. "I don't exactly know how to say this so you'll believe me, Charlie, but I'm going to try." He took a deep breath. "Admittedly, we were off to a rocky start because of my stupid behavior, but things have changed. I'm pretty sure I've fallen in love with you."

He put a finger on her lips when she started to speak. "No, let me finish. I'm also pretty sure that you love me," he added so tenderly that Charlie thought her heart would break in two. "But I have to be honest with you. I joined the Secret Service knowing full well the odds were against my being able to stay out of harm's way. I swore then to defend my country from foreign as well as domestic criminals and nothing has changed. I have to do my duty."

Charlie gazed into Mike's eyes. She felt guilty for having tried to persuade him to put safety above honor. When he'd returned her kiss, she'd almost believed his obvious desire for her would keep him with her tonight. She should have known better. Outside of her own father, Mike was the most honest and conscientious man she'd ever met. To insist he stay with her would only dishonor him in his own eyes.

She swallowed the lump in her throat. "Then go," she said gazing into his warm, concerned eyes, eyes that reflected his love for her. "But before you go promise me you'll take care of yourself. Promise me you'll call for backup if you need to. That you'll call me as soon as you can."

"I promise," he answered tenderly. "Let's go in.

Before I leave, I want to check the windows and doors.''

''Security always comes first,'' she said, choking on her forced laughter.

''No, sweetheart,'' he said with a tender look. ''You always come first.''

He took the house keys from Charlie's hand and opened the door. ''Wait right here in the kitchen while I check around. I particularly want to check the windows to make sure they're locked.''

To Charlie, every moment she waited for Mike seemed like an eternity. She tried to smile bravely when he came back.

''Everything's locked up tight,'' he said. ''Keep it that way.'' With one last quick kiss on the tip of her nose, he smiled into her eyes. ''I'll call you as soon as I can.''

AS HE DROVE down the highway to D.C., Mike forced himself not to look back. The irony of finding that the woman he loved with all his heart was also a woman whose life might depend on him wasn't lost on him.

Nor was the realization that he had to put aside that love for now and try to remain as objective about the situation as possible. He had to think methodically, follow his instincts and the information the commander had given him and keep Charlie in the background. Having her on his mind 24/7 was dangerous. Dangerous to him, and especially dangerous to her.

He studied the address Wade had given him. Columbus Square? He was acquainted with the area; it consisted of eclectic office buildings and was a shoppers' paradise. And a natural place for the Baronovian trade office. Wade had told him it was located on the fourth floor of the building.

With a possible game plan in mind, he checked out his surroundings. If the office were in the process of packing to move to larger quarters on Embassy Row, he reasoned, it would be simple to masquerade as an employee of the moving company to get inside.

If Petrov, as the head of the trade office, was supervising the move, it should be simple to identify him as the man Liz and Charlie had described. Granted, their recollections of the man were fuzzy, but one and one always made two in the end. He had to remain patient. If Petrov had a lot to lose when the trade office closed, he was his man.

He drove slowly until he spotted a moving truck.

Mike parked his unmarked car a block away and made his way through the lunch-hour traffic to Columbus Square. The moving company's truck was easy to identify. Knowing from experience that some people could be bought, he headed for the truck and tapped a mover on the shoulder.

"Like to make a C-note?"

The uniformed man cautiously eyed the bill Mike held between his finger tips. "Depends. What would I have to do?"

"Not much. Trade suits with me and stay out of sight for a few hours."

The man looked doubtfully at Mike's tailored black suit, then at his own dusty gray cotton jumpsuit. "You're sure?"

"I'm sure." Mike didn't mind losing the suit he wore almost as a uniform. Hell, he had several more at home hanging in his closet. Anyway he looked at it, the loss of the suit was worth it.

"So, what's in it for you?" The mover didn't look convinced.

Mike grinned. "I want to play a trick on the boss."

The man looked around him nervously. "Mine, or yours?"

"Neither," Mike answered. He added a twenty to sweeten his offer. "It's part of a surprise welcome party for a friend of mine. He's new to this country. I want to make him feel at home."

"Well…" The man hesitated, his eyes fastened on the bills. "How do I know you're legit?"

Mike put the bills back in his wallet and started toward another likely pigeon. "Forget it. I'll find someone else."

"No way!" The mover, whose name tag labeled

him as Joe Morales, held out his hand. "You saw me first."

"True." Mike gestured to the half-empty truck. "We can exchange clothing inside." He handed the mover the twenty and put the hundred-dollar bill back in his pocket. "You'll get the rest of the dough as soon as we switch and you disappear."

Morales shucked his jumpsuit in record time, traded it for Mike's suit and held out his hand for the C-note. "If I get busted," he warned, "I'm going to tell the cops you knocked me out and stole my clothes."

"Yeah, sure," Mike said dryly. "And you put on my suit because you were too modest to go around in your underwear."

Morales flushed. "Hell, this wasn't my idea, you know."

"Right. If you do get caught, tell it to the cops. But try to remember the idea is not to get noticed." Mike handed the man the money. "Get moving."

With Morales out of sight, Mike stepped into the jumpsuit, grabbed a padded blanket used to protect furniture and hoisted it on his shoulder. With his face partially obscured, he headed upstairs. He'd never kidded himself about the possibility of being in danger before and he didn't kid himself now. It would be a miracle if one of Joe's buddies didn't notice that his face and the name on the jumpsuit didn't match.

He plodded to the open freight elevator, closed the door before anyone could join him, punched the button for the fourth floor and prayed for the miracle.

By the time the elevator reached the fourth floor, a fine sheen of sweat covered Mike. He'd spent the past few minutes remembering rule number one in the Secret Service Handbook: "Never go it alone if you can help it. Always have a backup." And he'd promised Charlie to heed the warning.

Hell, it wouldn't be the first time he'd broken a rule or two. As for Charlie, he'd worry about her later.

"Hey, you over there!" a voice shouted. "Give me a hand with this bookcase!"

Relief swept over Mike. Whoever had called out obviously wasn't acquainted with Morales or he'd be calling for another kind of help.

"Sure." Mike dropped the padded blanket, gazed around the half-empty room and rubbed his aching back. "Jeez. How many rooms of furniture are there to go?"

"If you think this is a load, wait until you see the pileup on the other end of the job. The boss can't seem to make up her mind where she wants things to go."

"The boss is a woman?"

"Yeah, an Irine something or other. Can't make